D0149409

Rumors from the
boys' Room

Also by Rose Cooper

Gossip from the Girls' Room

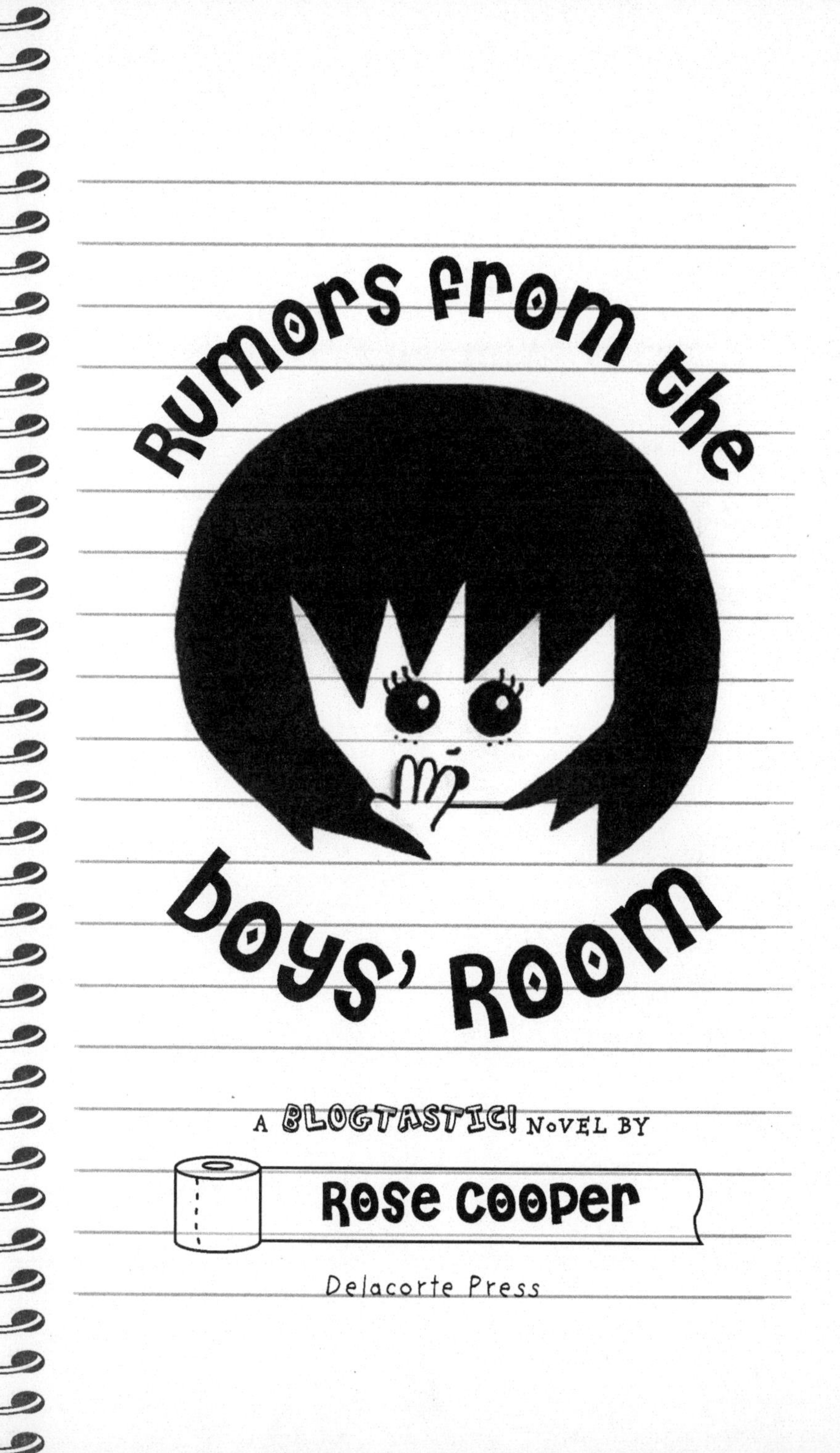
Rumors from the
boys' Room
A BLOGTASTIC! NOVEL BY
Rose Cooper
Delacorte Press

This is a work of fiction. Names, characters, places, and incidents either are the product of the author's imagination or are used fictitiously. Any resemblance to actual persons, living or dead, events, or locales is entirely coincidental.

 Published in the United States by Delacorte Press, an imprint of Random House Children's Books, a division of Random House, Inc., New York.

Delacorte Press is a registered trademark and the colophon is a trademark of Random House, Inc.

Visit us on the Web! randomhouse.com/kids

Educators and librarians, for a variety of teaching tools, visit us at randomhouse.com/teachers

Library of Congress Cataloging-in-Publication Data is available upon request.

ISBN 978-0-385-74084-5 (trade) — ISBN 978-0-375-98972-8 (lib. bdg.)

The text of this book is set in 12-point Providence-Sans.

Book design by Heather Daugherty

Printed in the United States of America
10 9 8 7 6 5 4 3 2 1

First Edition

Random House Children's Books supports the First Amendment and celebrates the right to read.

For my husband, Carl.

If you were a superhero, your name would be

Super-Incredible Awesome Man!

ACKNOWLEDGMENTS

Thank you to all the wonderful supporters of Blogtastic! An extra-special thanks to:

My brilliant brother, Brandon, who always believed in me. And who didn't mind growing up with such an incredibly awesome, amazingly phenomenal big sister with mad skills.

My BWFE (Best Writing Friends Ever), Amie Borst, Jen Daiker, and Candace Granger. Aside from your sparkly blogs and the ability to make me laugh (to the point of tears), your creativity and talent inspire me.

Rosemary Stimola, my sensational agent, and the super-fabulous team at Random House, expecially designer Heather Daugherty, publicity assistant Lauren Donovan, and editor extraordinaire Wendy Loggia.

Rose Green, for sharing your knowledge of

everything German and allowing me to pick your brain.

And all the readers of the Blogtastic series. You guys are fantastic, and I love all the email and comments!

CONSIDER THIS A WARNING!!!

This is not just any notebook. This is still my super-secret Pre-Blogging Notebook, with all my innermost private thoughts. Well, until they become public when I post ~~all~~ some of them on my almost-popular blog. And just because I, Sofia Becker, need to jot down all the juiciness I hear does not mean I'm forgetful. Even if my brain sometimes gets stage fright (which, BTW, is totally normal for a sixth grader). I'm just taking extra-special precautions to make sure all the super-important details do not get mixed up before I actually blog about what happened. That might cause confusion.

And once my anonymous blog becomes popular (it's so close, I can smell it), I will post totally cool things about me and my friends that will make us way cool and popular too. Especially since mine is one of the most fabtastic blogs on the school site.

Even if Mr. Anderson, the newspaper advisor and blog monitor, has to keep reminding me of certain posting rules that I sometimes break. But only because it slips my mind due to excited participation.

So to keep this notebook super-secret, I've cleverly disguised it as a boring, ordinary notebook. And NOBODY knows of its very existence.

Well, except for my BFF, Nona Bows. She's THE one exception to every rule I make up.

By the way, if you are reading this and your name isn't Nona Bows, you are a snoopy person and have somehow made it past my precautions. Or I have lost my notebook for the second time—and you should've immediately placed it (unread!) in the lost and found and not in your hands. Even if you are a janitor. Or pretending to be one.

Like that one time Mia St. Claire's dad found my notebook

So now my professionally trained attack parrot, Sam Sam, has been alerted to your nosiness. If I were you, I would put this notebook down and slooowly back away. . . .

01

It was a total accident! I swear! I didn't mean to see two of my teachers talking all secret-like. And I didn't mean to hear what they were talking all secret-like about either.

If something is whispered, it's an instant secret.

Just because I was kinda tiptoeing back to my locker after school since I'd forgotten my cell phone and was trying not to make my presence known does NOT mean I was being sneaky in any way. In fact, the old Sofia Becker would've gossiped. But the new Sofia Becker has decided that gossip is best left to the columnists and not the awesomeness of what is called my blog.

Other things the old Sofia would've done

So being all new now, I only blog about things I know are true and hear about for myself. That way I know the information comes from a trusty source: me!

Even though the hallways were as empty as my dessert plate on chocolate cake night and any sound could be heard pretty easily, I couldn't hear the exact words the teachers were saying.

So this gave me more reason to tiptoe closer.

still not sneaky-ish

The news sounded pretty exciting even though one of the teachers seemed way less than excited.

Teacher 1: The foreign exchange student should be here soon.

Teacher 2: Yes, yes.

Teacher 1: This is our first foreign exchange student in ten years!

Teacher 2: Yes, yes.

I wonder if all conversations with Teacher 2 are like that.

After my non-sneaky, non-eavesdropping ears heard the rest of the secret-like conversational exchange, I did the only thing I could. I rushed home and blogged about it.

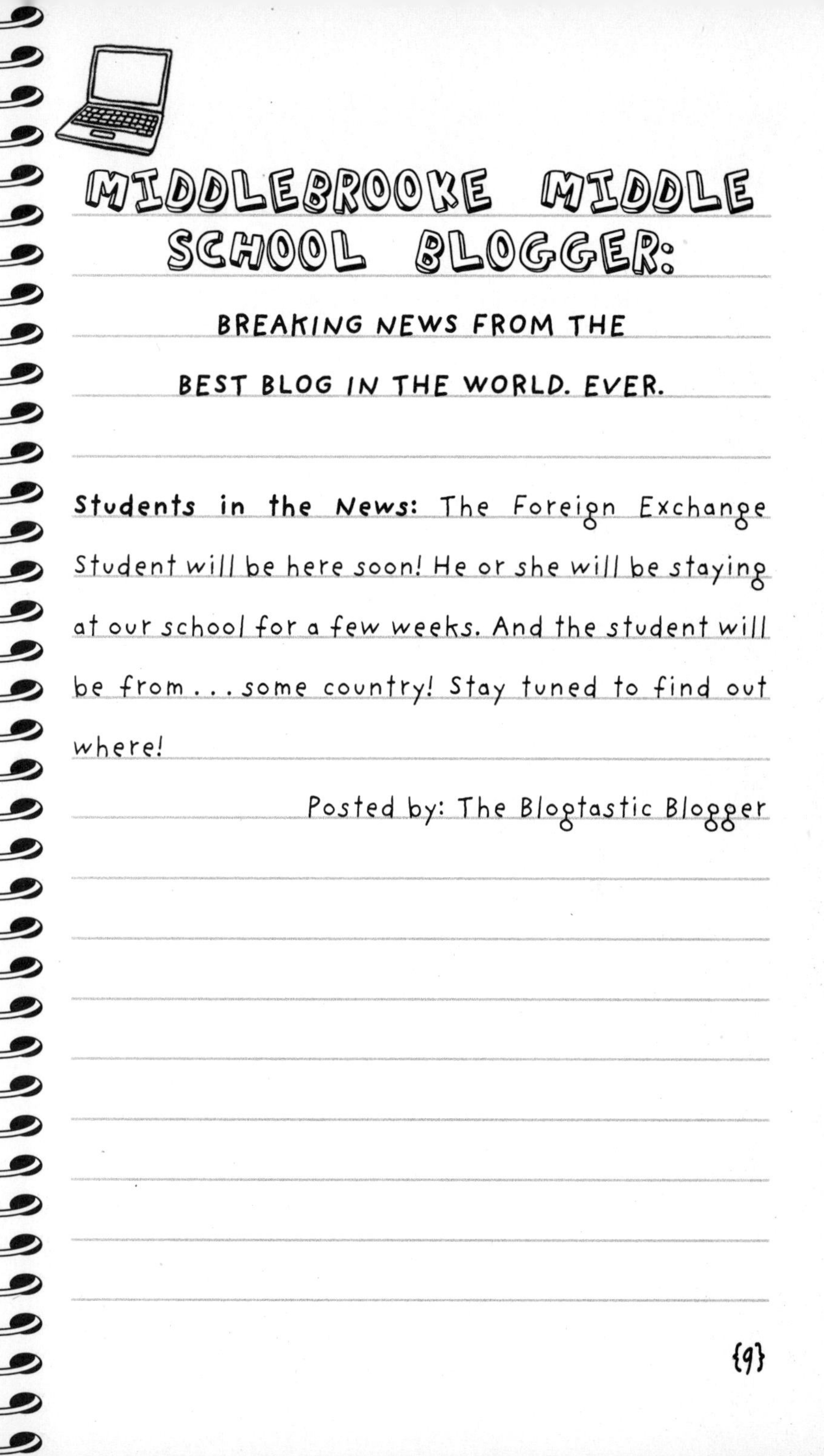

MIDDLEBROOKE MIDDLE SCHOOL BLOGGER:

BREAKING NEWS FROM THE
BEST BLOG IN THE WORLD. EVER.

Students in the News: The Foreign Exchange Student will be here soon! He or she will be staying at our school for a few weeks. And the student will be from . . . some country! Stay tuned to find out where!

Posted by: The Blogtastic Blogger

WEDNESDAY 02

BEFORE SCHOOL

I always meet Nona at her locker, but since I'm always there before she is, I have to hang out alone until she shows. I try to act like I'm doing something super-important once the hallways begin to fill with students.

Some wisdom I've picked up: waiting and looking bored makes you unimportant because people should be waiting for _you_, not the other way around. And it also pushes you down the popularity meter like 5 points.

Other things that push you down the popularity meter

Wearing a costume. When it's not Halloween.

Begging for candy. When it's not Halloween.

Having a weird obsession for all things Halloween. When it's not Halloween.

If I tell Nona to meet me at my locker in the mornings instead and I just "happen" to be late, I could very quite possibly blow the top off the popularity meter in no time.

Except Nona has a habit of being easily entertained and nobody would probably even realize she was waiting.

Just then, Andrew, my biggest forever crush (and THE most popular boy in all of sixth grade), walks by and waves. At me!

Okay. So maybe Andrew didn't want to yell out my name and make things all awkward. Still, I felt like my heart was pulled out of my chest.

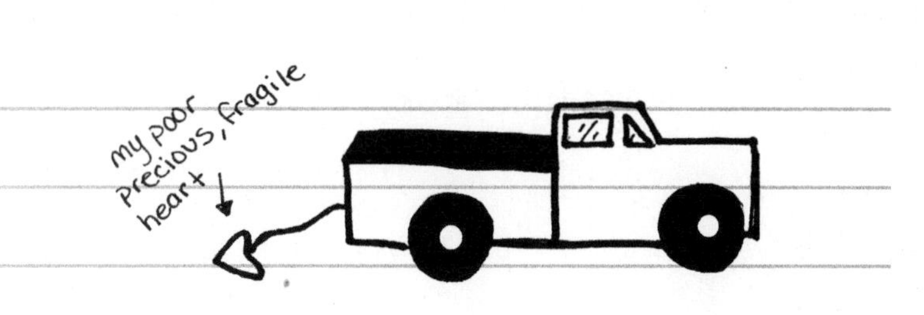

And dragged behind a pickup truck.
Over a ton of sharp rocks.

Nona shows up (finally!) and gives me her weird one-raised-eyebrow look and says, "Why are you staring at your wrist?"

I give her my scrunched-nose isn't-it-obvious look and say back, "I'm pretending to see what time it is while I wait for you."

"But you don't have a watch," she points out.

"That's why I said PRETEND." Sigh.

Sometimes friendships are exhausting.

Nona asks me why I'm at school so early and I remind her that since my mother went from part-time to full-time embarrassment as Teacher Mom at our school (and to über-embarrassment as Pregnant

Mom), she thinks it's "cool" to ride together in the morning. I convinced her that since we only live two blocks away, a kid like me ought to get as much exercise as possible by riding my bike. So we compromised.

I will ride with her to school every Wednesday. And on rainy days. And on really hot, humid sweaty days.

Ways of getting to school IF it were based on popularity

Expensive, fancy-like car. Probably with its own driver. Definitely for the Popular Pretties. Like Mia. Ugh.

Bike. For normal kids, like Nona and me. Except we will soon be populars, so it doesn't really count.

Pogo stick.
For the wannabe friends of the soon-to-be populars. Or the highly energetic. Like Alice.

Cartwheels.
For the I-wish-I-were unpopulars, because they don't even rank. These kids usually wear mismatched socks or inside-out shirts.

Alice Ava, our newish friend and Nona's locker neighbor, arrives and is way too happy as she gets books from her locker.

"Hey, guys!"

I barely rolled out of bed and she has enough energy to run a marathon. Way too early for that.

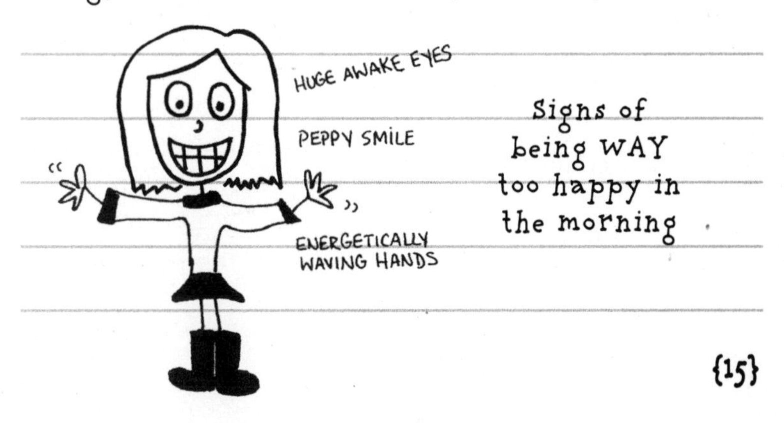

Signs of being WAY too happy in the morning

Alice, like me and Nona, is an unpopular. Although we are soon destined to be populars since I'm the anonymous Blogtastic Blogger and the blog is gaining more popularity, which means I can soon start blogging cool things about us, which will make us way popular!

I think Alice has wanted to hang out with us recently because she senses our deep-down übercoolness.

Or maybe she's a vampire who can smell our closeness to popularity.

When Alice first confided in us about her distaste for Mia and Penelope and all those other popular and snooty girls, I had to give her a high five and call her our new best friend.

I so love myself. and bunnies. and rainbows. Oh, and my cute little bow.

ugh. Her bow is so last season.

Popular Pretty vs. Super Snooty

Even though Mia St. Claire is at the top of the popularity scale, she's at the top of my annoyance meter.

REASONS WHY MIA IS THE MOST ANNOYING GIRL IN ALL OF MIDDLEBROOKE MIDDLE SCHOOL:

Her hair smells like fresh strawberries. (I only know this

because one time she walked too close to me and I was forced to sniff.)

She's super-rich. I suspect she buys her friends, which makes her fake-popular.

She has the ability to cast spells on boys and make them like her. (Don't worry, Andrew, I'll find a cure and save you!)

There are MANY more reasons I could name, but then I'd be stuck writing for like a week just to list them all.

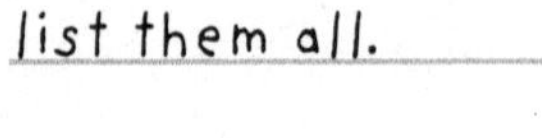

Mia and Penelope were once what you would call total besties. Now they're more like frenemies, ever since Penelope told everyone about Mia's secret crush when she swore she wouldn't.

Or maybe it was me who accidentally overheard and told. I kind of forget the details.

So now Mia has declared some girl Maddie as her new bestie, which automatically bumped Maddie up to number two on the popularity meter. I really don't get it. I mean, what does Maddie have that the rest of us don't?

Besides the longest hair I've ever seen.

I bet Mia is just using Maddie for her hair. After all, the possibilities are endless.

I will now need to teach my awesome pet parrot, Sam Sam, some new words.

-Long hair is unfun!
-mad maddie!
squawk!

I'm glad Penelope was replaced, though. She's been out to get me ever since I (accidentally) squirted cow eyeball juice on her new outfit during a dissection project in science class. She got me detention, so you would think we were even, but no. Mean people like Penelope never. Give. Up.

STUDY HALL

We're supposed to be studying. Or doing assignments. But in my case, if no one was next to me I could be blogging. Of course, no such luck. Long-Legged Lenny is sitting next to me and he takes up just about all the possible legroom under our table. I know it's not his fault that he's overgrown and tall enough to be a superstar basketball player, but still.

While I pretend to study, Nona nudges me and tells me about her total non-fun idea that starts with an "L" and ends with a "T." And it might have an "IS" in the middle.

In third grade I officially named Nona The Most Organized Person Ever. She makes lists for everything.

She even makes lists for lists.

Nona decided that "we" (meaning Nona) should make a list of the possible countries that the FES (Foreign Exchange Student) might come from.

To save time, I just Googled her a map.

AFTER SCHOOL

As I'm walking to meet my mom, I hear a parent talking to one of the teachers about the FES in a hushed voice. Like it's a big secret or something. And I know it was about the FES because they actually mention which country he's coming from! Yes, it's a boy!

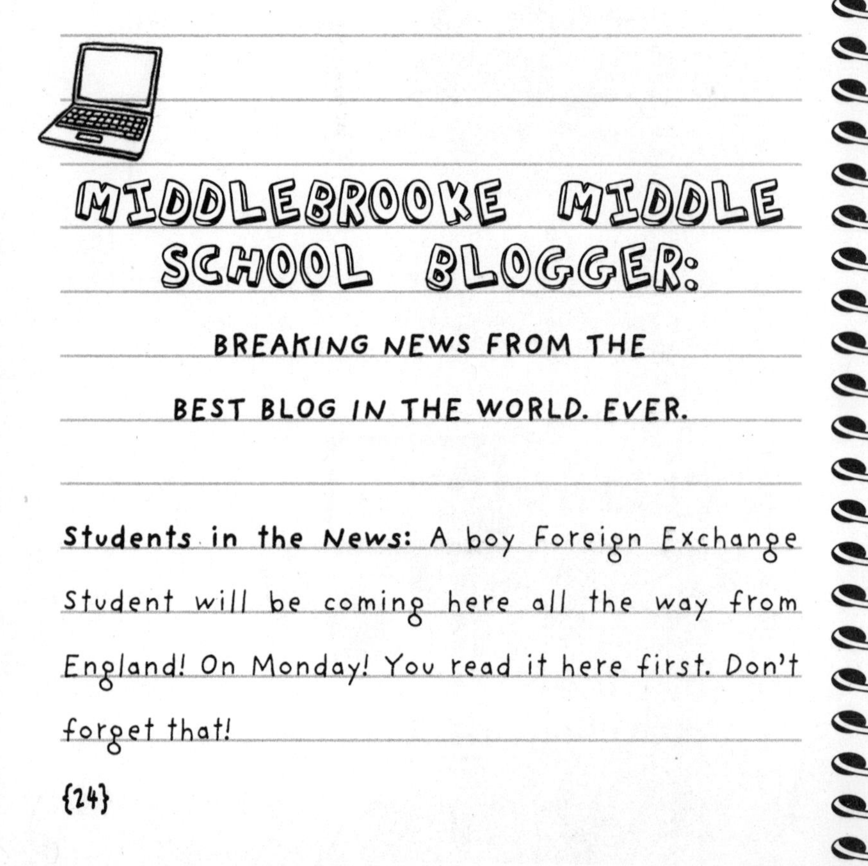

MIDDLEBROOKE MIDDLE SCHOOL BLOGGER:

BREAKING NEWS FROM THE BEST BLOG IN THE WORLD. EVER.

Students in the News: A boy Foreign Exchange Student will be coming here all the way from England! On Monday! You read it here first. Don't forget that!

Also, Mia St. Claire was seen waiting a long time by someone's locker looking very, very bored. Did I mention for a really long time?

Teachers in the News: Mrs. Becker is having weird pregnant cravings, which include eating the cafeteria food!

Posted by: The Blogtastic Blogger

Blog Comment by Advisor Mr. A: Remember the rule about not using full names?

Besides eating cafeteria food willingly, my mom is also doing other bizarre things. On purpose. Like today she saw me in the hall and instead of her normal Teacher Mom embarrassment, she did this non-normal Teacher Mom embarrassment.

She waved and said hi. Without yelling.

Usually Mom is super-loud. But this time she didn't call me Sofia or honey or remind everyone in school that she's my mom. So really, it's like she could've been talking to anyone. If everyone didn't already know who she was.

And if my mom-embarrassment reflexes hadn't already kicked in.

THE BUZZ AROUND SCHOOL . . .

Everyone is talking about the new FES like we're expecting royalty or something. I wonder if being an FES equals instant popularity. Or if being friends with an FES equals instant popularity.

Other things that SHOULD equal instant popularity

book nerds

milk mustaches

STUDY HALL

It was my turn to show Nona how lists are really supposed to be done. So I told her that we need to pick the funnest countries. Ever. And the one that "we" (meaning me) think would be super-fun for obvious reasons, besides knowing that the FES is coming from England, is . . . England!

Other countries that would be fun

Italy.
Because they have my favorite salad dressing. Ever.

China. Since I love panda bears best of all.

France. Seriously? French fries are the bomb!

LUNCHTIME DILEMMA

So here's the deal. The FES is SUPPOSED to be here Monday, but now everyone is saying he will be here tomorrow. Why tomorrow? Because some Bloghead boy is spreading the word. I know my information is very accurate, so it has to be the new boy blogger who is wrong. And why does he have to blog about the same stuff as me?

I know the FES will be here on Monday because Aaron told Melita, who told Penelope (I heard them in the hallway), so really, it's like Aaron practically told me himself because Aaron is very trustworthy (he says he never lies).

Signs of a liar

hair pulling crying

AT MY HOUSE

After Nona and I finished our homework (boring!), I had a wonderful, terrific idea!

I decided we should practice our British accents so that the FES will feel very comfortable and will want to be our friend. I Google everything I can about Britishisms. Nona asks me when this stuff was actually written because it could be WAY outdated and the FES will laugh at us.

Outdated? Even Nona should know that language doesn't get outdated. Ever.

Nona was ever-so-slightly offended that I told her she was wrong.

In England, instead of saying goodbye, you say Cheerio. How cool is that? Cheerios are my runner-up favorite cereal! I think America should use a cereal name as a greeting. But why would Cheerios be the most popular? I'm going to use my favorite instead—Cocoa Puffs!

I suggested Nona use Trix. She said that stuff is for kids. Besides, it would sound like she was pranking someone. I told her she is totally missing out.

Nona's missing!

Giggle

Sometimes Sam Sam chooses to only repeat certain words. Go figure.

Oh well, more fun for me. I decide to up the fun factor and even blog like a Brit!

MIDDLEBROOKE MIDDLE SCHOOL BLOGGER:

BREAKING NEWS FROM THE MOST BRILLIANT BLOG IN THE WORLD. EVER.

Students in the News: P went absolutely barmy in the cafeteria when she spilled cranberry juice on her posh white frock.

J.L. had a fit when she was late to one of her classes. It's time to put on your big-girl blouse! Everybody is late at some point.

To the Bloghead chap who just started a blog: Use your bonce and stop being a nosy parker. Blog about your own stuff, not mine.

This post is totally ace. Bob's your uncle.

Posted by: The Blogtastic Blogger

Blog Comment by Anon Student 1: I have an uncle named Bob too!

Blog Comment by Anon Student 2: Who's Bloghead? Now I want to see what that blog is about.

FRIDAY

04

The FES is here today, which means Aaron was wrong! Actually, I bet it was Penelope who lied. If she lies about wearing brand-name clothes (like those fake Pradas she has on today), I'm willing to bet she's a full-time liar.

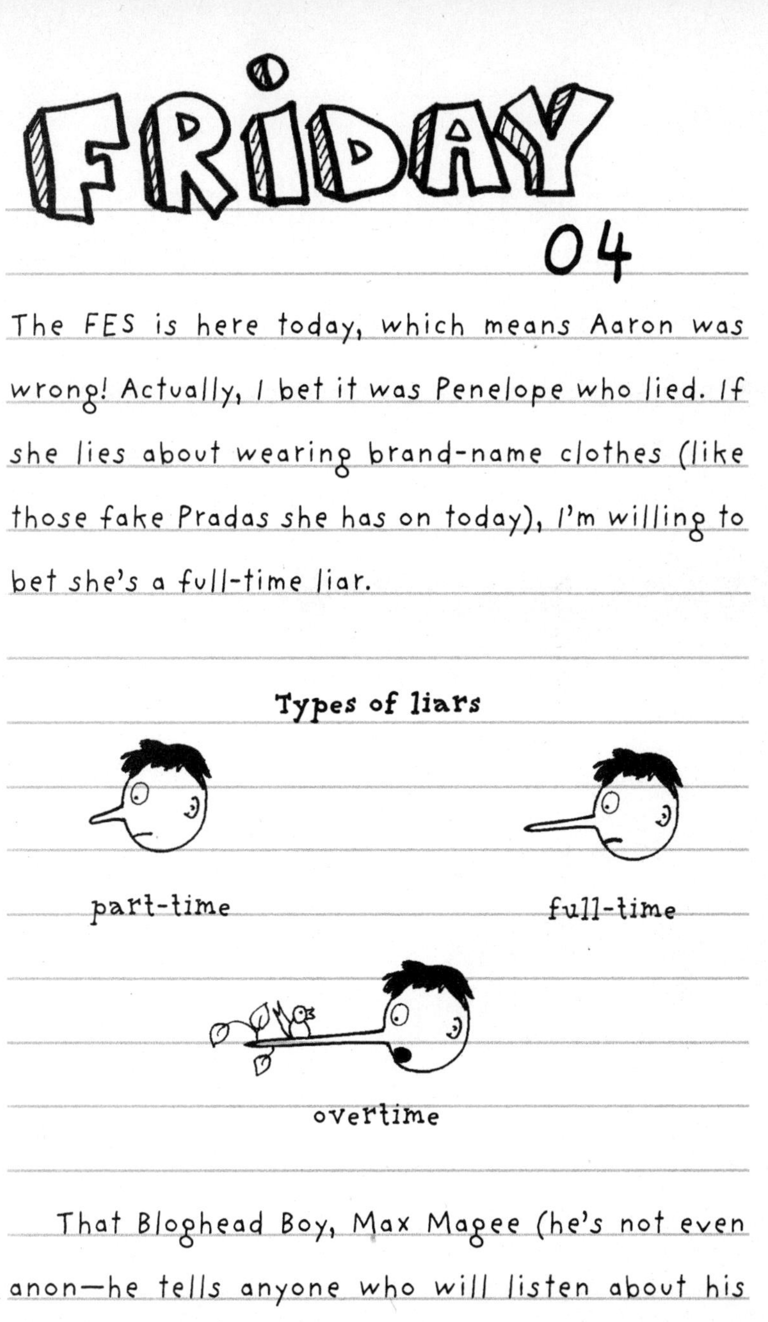

That Bloghead Boy, Max Magee (he's not even anon—he tells anyone who will listen about his blog), was right, which makes me really not like him even more now. And where is he getting his information? But the worst part is, I didn't even know who the FES was until Mr. Allen introduced him in geography, aka zombie class. Dressed in just a T-shirt and jeans, he doesn't even look like an FES.

Wait, where's the British accent? "Goo-ten Tag" isn't British.

I raise my hand (or more like my arm shoots up so fast I almost dislocate my shoulder) and I ask, "Where are you from?"

"Berlin, Germany," Lukas says happily.

I turn around and whisper to Nona, "How can this be?"

Nona: Your ears overheard wrong.

Me: But I was right there. I heard Mrs. Harrison talking.

Nona: You mean Mrs. Harrison the English teacher?

Me: Uh, yeah. So what?

Nona: Are you sure she wasn't talking about English? Like her English class and not England the country?

I turn back around in my seat. Whatever.

Non-English FES, aka Lukas from Germany, is actually really super-cute.

Actually, I declare him the second-cutest boy in

all of Middlebrooke (Andrew's the first, of course!), which knocks Joey down to third.

He wears socks with sandals, but because of his cuteness, that can totally be overlooked.

On a side note, Lukas has the nicest-looking eyes. Ever. I notice this as he turns in my direction and looks directly at . . . Nona.

And Nona actually blushes! And smiles. And giggles. She mimics a whole total act of girliness that I never thought I'd witness.

Lukas and Nona lock eyes like it's almost

magical. I mean, I can almost see the fairy dust and sparkles between them. Why doesn't that happen when Andrew looks at me? Does that ever happen when Mia looks at him?

I wouldn't mind if bombs
exploded when Mia looks at him.

As much as I hated to, I had to break the five-second hypnotic connection for Nona's sake. Or else she would've been a goner for sure.

the only way I could think of

Nona: What are you doing?

Me: I'm saving you. You're welcome.

Nona: What are you talking about?

Me: I was protecting you. You can't stare into his eyes like that.

Nona: I wasn't staring into anyone's eyes.

Me: Yes, you were. And if you do that again, you'll turn into stone.

Nona: That's Medusa, not Lukas, you dork!

Me: Aha! So you do admit it!

Nona: I don't admit anything.

Me: Guilty as charged.

Nona (shrugs): Whatever.

I'm pretty certainly positive that Nona has fallen under a Lukas spell, because she's not making much sense. And apparently, she's not the only one. Mia St. Claire seems less absorbed in herself (at the moment) and more into Lukas.

The good thing: She's less interested in Andrew.

The bad thing: She wants to steal Nona's crush. Again. Nona's heart was just recently repaired; she can't be heartbroken again. And as much as I want Mia to leave Andrew alone, I want even more for her to leave Lukas alone.

It's a good thing I have a plan!

The weekend goes by so fast it's like one huge blur. Half the time I can't remember if it's Saturday or Sunday. So to save my brain from having to think too much, I just call it Sunturday. Pretty clever, right?

Nona insisted I go to her house this weekend. And with all the Mom strangeness going on at home, she didn't have to ask twice.

MOM WEIRDNESS

I totally hate to admit it, but Mom HAS been acting way weirder than normal.

She says it's because of the pregnancy. Poor Mom. Lately she seems to be exhausted all the time. But like the non-normal kind of exhausted.

And then she falls asleep in random places.

Like a few days ago Dad and I were looking everywhere for her. Her snores finally gave away her secret sleeping place. In the corner of the kitchen. On the ground. Next to the fridge.

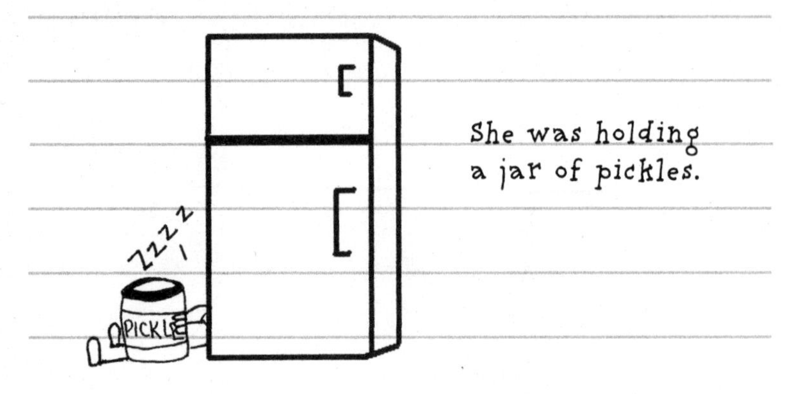

She was holding a jar of pickles.

Teaching a Spanish class can't be easy either.

"I had the class watch Spanish movies today," Mom announced on Friday.

I'm sure the volume was up loud (very loud!) to drown out her snores (another pregnancy symptom).

NONA'S HOUSE OF THE WEIRD KIND

I've exchanged one weirdness for another. And I think Nona's mom has been taken over by aliens or something. Because when she opens the door, she doesn't look like Nona's mom at all.

big hair

headband

weird shirt

legwarmers

And when she opens her mouth, she speaks a language that I've never heard, and it makes me wonder what country she's been secretly visiting.

Gnarly!

Don't have a cow!

Gag me with a spoon!

I ask Mrs. Bows if she's joking around and she says, "Not even!" Then she says we're going to have a "wicked cool time" and that it will be "totally tubular" and then she says, "Word to your mother."

I look from Nona to her crazy mom, then back to Nona. I wonder if she's aware of her mom's condition. Maybe Mrs. Bows is pregnant too.

Me: So, what's going on?

Nona: My mom is on her way to

some flashback school reunion party.

Me: That's weird.

Nona: What's weird is that her clothes and the way she's talking are totally eighties.

Me: Um, okay.

Nona: I wanted to show you how OUTDATED this stuff is.

Me: And your point?

Nona: My point? You said on Thursday at 4:12 p.m. that language doesn't get outdated. So my point is . . . I'm NEVER WRONG.

Have I ever mentioned how exhausting friendships can be? Especially ones with girls named Nona.

I trap Lukas on the way to the boys' room between classes. And by trap I mean stop. And by stop I mean I jump in front of him so he has to acknowledge me. And the look on his face is either surprise or fear.

Maybe both?

I say hi all nice and sweetly so he knows that I mean him no harm. He kinda laughs and then says, "Aren't you friends with the flowery girl?"

Flowery girl? Oh, of course. Nona always wears a flower in her hair. I never thought of her as very flowery, though.

I tell him yes and ask him if he likes her. He smiles and nods. I want to jump up and down and cheer. I got to him before Mia! Since I'm on a roll, I ask him a few more questions.

Me: So you're crushing on Nona, huh?

Lukas: Crushing?

Me: You have a crush on her.

Lukas: I'm not sure.

Me: Oh. Are you seeing anybody?

Lukas: I see lots of people.

Me: But you like Nona?

Lukas: Yes, she's cute.

Well, he likes her but doesn't have a crush on her and probably has lots of girlfriends but . . . whatever. Then I ask him THE most important question:

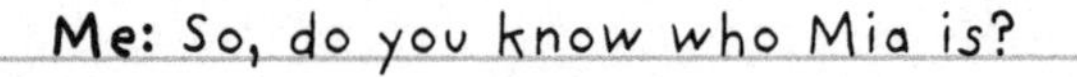

Me: So, do you know who Mia is?

Lukas: Of course! I live with her.

Lukas: Mia's family is hosting me while I stay here in America.

Me: No way. (I say this more to myself, but he hears me and laughs. Even though this is so not funny!)

Lukas: You're friends with her?

Me: No way! I mean, not really. So, how do you like school here? (Changing the subject usually works.)

Lukas: It's cool, but weird. At my

school in Germany, we always stay in the same class and the teachers come to us for the different subjects.

Yuck. That's too much like elementary school all over again. And trust me, getting stuck with Mia ALL DAY is just . . . there aren't words to explain.

Sophia and Mia back in first grade

Not much has changed.

And that new best friend of hers, Maddie? Yeah, she is way annoying too.

I think hair flinging is a side effect of popularity.

RUMORS FROM THE BOYS' ROOM

I leave to go to my locker, and Lukas heads to the boys' room. Since my locker is just around the corner from the boys' bathroom, I can't help but spy on him. Well, if you can call it that. Really, it's more like just peeking around the corner.

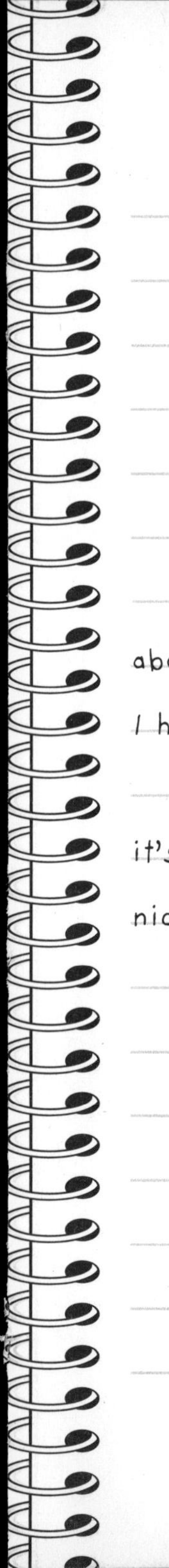

And following him with my eyes.

AFTER SCHOOL

Nona comes over thinking we're going to talk about the new FES and plan my next blog entry, but I have a surprise for her!

Since we can exchange students now, I think it's the perfect time to exchange Mia for a way nicer girl. Minus all the prettiness and popularness.

Isn't it way obvious what I'm doing? I have Mia St. Claire's box ready to go, and it shouldn't take more than, what, a couple of hours to ship her to another country?

Okay, so I throw a couple of granola bars in, just in case she gets hungry, and poke a few extra airholes in the box.

And then my biggest crush since nearly almost forever, Andrew, will notice me way more with her out of the picture, and Nona's heart will be saved.

Ship out, Mia, Squawk!

Nona points out that we will probably also want to exchange TGBE (The Grossest Boy Ever, aka Scott Barley) for a less-gross boy and Penelope for a less-mean girl who wears a smaller bow in her hair.

TUESDAY 08

WORST MORNING EVER

The bell rings for homeroom, and even though I'm standing right there with her, Nona grabs her book, slams her locker, and takes off. WITHOUT ME!

Hello? Remember me, your BFF? The one who is willing to ship out Mia for you and only you (if we had money for the actual shipping)? I'm so speechless I just stand there stunned as the hallway empties and my brain goes numb.

To make a horrible situation even more horrible, Penelope and her group walk by. Penelope has a smirk on her face. "Nona sure left in a hurry. Did you forget to take a shower?" she says.

She laughs, and her friends look at me and then hold their noses. I grit my teeth, wishing I could think of a good comeback. But since I can't, I give them the infamous Evil Sofia Glare.

if looks could injure

This area left blank intentionally due to angriness and the inability to actually write without breaking my pen in half with my super-girly kung fu gripness.

132-1/2 MINUTES LATER, AFTER COOLING DOWN . . .

RUMORS FROM THE BOYS' ROOM

Okay, so I'm not stalking Lukas in any way, but I stand by my locker waiting for him to come out of the boys' room (I just might have happened to see him go in). So when he does, I stop him. And this time by stop him I mean I just call out his name and wait for him to stop.

So I ask him if he heard anything in the boys' room just now. You know, since I maybe kinda sort of saw Andrew go in there too . . . but I was in no way stalking him either. I can't help that the boys' room is in my direct line of vision.

you know, if I had X-ray glasses and could see through the wall

Disappointingly, Lukas says, "Nothing." I feel like I'm about to cry or something, because I'm one of those types of girls, and I think he can see it, because his eyes get this certain look of terror.

But then he says, "Oh, wait! There is one thing."

And I can immediately feel all the tension in my face melt away and instantly be replaced by a smile. "ONE thing?" I whisper.

"There's this boy who I think likes you."

OMG!

"Who? Who? Who?" I so don't care that I sound like an owl.

Lukas doesn't say anything for a minute, and that drags on the suspense for way too long.

"Was it Andrew?" I ask.

"Yes! That's who it was!" he says.

At that very exact precise moment, which I will never forget for the rest of my life (or until I get really old and have no choice), I feel like nothing else in the world matters.

Then Lukas asks me if I'll switch seats with him in Mr. Allen's class. You know, so he can sit next to Nona.

Obviously Nona isn't speaking to me for some reason, so it's pretty much like I'm not sitting next to her anyway, so I agree. Lukas winks at me, then leaves.

Mia conveniently walks up to me at that same moment (what a stalker!) and says, "If he winked at you, he didn't mean it. He's still getting used to wearing contacts."

I can't tell if she's trying to be nice or rubbing it in my face.

Mia's secret signs of meanness

"cutesy" bow used as a distraction before hypnotizing you with her beauty

scented hair that viciously attacks the nose

huge innocent eyes that aggressively judge you a look of shock when anyone suspects her ambush of meanness

WEDNESDAY

09

MORNING MOM MADNESS

My morning started with Mom driving us to school. Actually, it started with her trying to sing <u>while</u> driving us to school. Have you ever heard a pregnant mom try to sing? It's the worst sound in the world. It sounds like fingernails screeching down a chalkboard.

or a cat in
a washing machine
on the spin cycle

I almost doze off from officially having Zombiness.

Geography,
aka
zombie class

Zombiness (zom-bee-ness), noun: Dying of boredom, then coming back alive. Only happens in Mr. Allen's geography class, due to his monotone voice and lack of interesting subjects to teach.

It looks like Lukas is prone to Zombiness too.

Maddie even asks him why he looks so tired, as if it's not completely obvious. She's probably just thinking of reasons to talk to him.

Lukas whispers back to her, "My school was only from eight a.m. to noon. Not used to these longer days."

What? Four-hour school days? I'm so moving to Germany!

Nona still isn't talking to me, otherwise I would tell her how awesome the German schools are, although I'm sure she overheard Lukas. But the point is, she's <u>still</u> on some sort of talking strike. That's like Mia St. Claire going on a bow strike.

So there's really only one way to get Nona's attention. And I have to do it the first chance I get. I jot down a quick note for her, being so completely sensitive to whatever mood she's going through right now.

Hey, what's up, butt head??

But there is one—make that two HUGE obstacles that sit right in the very way of my note delivery. And their names are Mia St. Claire and Penelope. I have two possible routes. I must choose carefully.

Option #1: Give note to Penelope, the meanest girl ever, who will have to hand note to TGBE to give to Nona. While in transit, note is liable to get ripped (by Penelope's fake claws) and boogered on (by TGBE).

Option #2: Give note to Mia St. Claire, aka Miss Popular (gag!), who will have to hand note to Andrew, my total crush, to give to Nona. While note is in transit, Mia's hand is liable to touch Andrew's. Actually touch! Need I say more? Or even worse, they might make eye contact and Mia will put a hypnotic spell on Andrew and he will have a forever crush on her.

So I pick the only option I can.

Option #3: none of the above.

I fold the note into a paper airplane, and as soon as Mr. Allen turns his back to the room, I throw it straight at Nona's head.

How was I supposed to know the airplane would do a bunch of loopy loops and crash into the teacher's butt?

I don't think anyone saw me actually throw the note, because when Mr. Allen asks who called him a butthead, the whole class laughs but nobody points a finger at me. But when class is over, Mia St. Claire whispers, "Pretty gutsy." Then she flings her hair into my line of smell and I'm forced to catch a whiff of the fresh sunny lemons that she must have washed her hair with.

Other kinds of shampoos Mia probably has stashed away

But there is one person who for sure knew it was me and I totally want to do a happy dance. Because Nona Bows actually ends her talking strike long enough to say, "I'll be over at your house to do homework."

Or maybe she took a vow of silence
to become a mime for drama?

AFTER SCHOOL

Nona comes over to do homework AFTER I've finished mine, which means she just so obviously wants the answers. Which is really not smart because she's the one who's a straight-A student.

Another thing that's so strangely weird is that she's acting like everything is fine and normal and nothing is wrong.

So when she says, "Let's do something fun," I put my foot down.

And for the first time, I think in forever, Nona actually looks sad. Like an actual tear might even escape from one of her tear ducts. She looks down at her lap and whispers:

Nona: Barney died.

Me: Your grandpa?

Nona: (shakes head)

Me: Uncle?

Nona: (shakes head)

Me: Nephew?

Nona: (shakes head)

Me: Who? Your great-grandpa? Great-uncle? Cousin? Friend of the family? Mailman?

Nona: My dog.

Now it was time for me to shake my head. Nona doesn't HAVE a dog. I tell her this since she seems to have forgotten.

Maybe she watched a movie
and got confused or something.

She tells me she adopted a dog. And she didn't

even have to go to court to do it. All she did was feed him every time he came around her house, which was all the time. But for the last few days he hasn't shown up.

Me: Your mom let you have a dog?

Nona: She didn't _let_ me. She said as long as he stayed outside it would be fine. You know, after she determined him to not be a threat.

Nona's mom has dog issues because of her childhood past.

Me: How'd you come up with the name Barney? Did he have dog tags?

Nona: No. It just sounded cool.

Even though I think Nona made a bad choice of dog names, I am still the awesome friend that I always am and I tell her it's entirely possible that Barney's not dead. He probably just went to someone else's house for food.

Nona says no way, because she puts his favorite food outside and sits on the porch every night calling his name. Maybe he forgot his name, I suggest.

Like when my grandpa forgot his name.
And how to eat an apple.

10

Nona seems in a better mood now that she's talked about Barney. I tell her she should ask her parents for a real pet of her own, something besides that creepy lizard she keeps in her room. She says she's given up on dogs so she will probably become a cat person instead.

She asks me why Lukas is sitting next to her in class instead of me. I remind her that she was giving me the silent treatment, so I gave her space. And that I don't have any control over who sits next to her. And that Lukas might have asked to switch seats with me.

I notice that Nona talks to Lukas a lot more too. In class. When we clearly shouldn't be talking. And just because she and I used to talk when I sat next to her, well, that's completely different. And just because I ask her what they talk about doesn't mean I'm being snoopy because I'm jealous.

Me: So what are you and Lukas always talking about? I don't think you even used to talk to me that much before.

Nona (shrugs): He tells me about his old school and stuff in Germany.

Me: He is super-cute, you know.

Nona: He's really nice too. Did you know he taught me ten ways to say thank you in German?

Me: No, but he's cute. Like Andrew.

Nona: Sure. But he's interesting also. And he taught me that a cell phone is called a handy.

I think my cell phone should be called an un-handy because it never has a signal in emergencies.

THE UN-FUNNESS OF WHAT IS CALLED A SCHOOL PROJECT

Our guidance counselor talked to our class today about building our character traits and assigned us a project to help us develop those traits. So now we have to think of something that helps us build leadership.

Nona raised her hand to make sure she was the first to claim her topic. "I will lead the school in a peaceful protest to change the cafeteria menu. Or at least make the food edible."

Good thing she claimed that one. I'm sure there were a lot of people who wanted to snatch up that idea. Not.

"I," said Penelope snootily, "will start a name-brand clothing donation collection for the homeless."

I was holding back laughter, until I heard Mia St. Claire giggle.

Ha Ha
Ha SNORT!
Ha
SNORT!

A few other people laughed too, but guess who Penelope gave the evil eye to? Yep, me. Luckily, I only had to feel uncomfortable for a few seconds, because Mia went on to explain her project idea next.

"I will put together a group of girls to give makeovers to the elderly, and collect donations for makeup," said Mia.

Then, just like Penelope, Mia looked in my

direction, and she said, "And I only need help from girls who actually know how to wear makeup."

I could so totally wear makeup. If I wanted to. Well, on my next birthday. Dad said I can wear lip gloss then. That counts, right?

Alice said she would be in charge of starting a book club. I'm not sure what book clubs do besides read a lot, so how can you take charge of that?

As soon as I heard Andrew's voice, my head automatically spun in his direction.

So fast, actually, that I nearly get whiplash.

I thought I heard him say, "I'm choosing a lead role where Sofia and I will have to spend a lot of time together." But really, he said, "I'm class president so I'm already in a leadership role."

I was close.

Luckily, hearing about everyone else's ideas gave me the inspiration I so desperately needed.

Why should our exchange of things be limited to just people?

We should be able to exchange other things too, like animals! So my project will so cleverly be an Awesome Pet Exchange! Or APE for short.

It will be so cool seeing what it's like to have a different pet. My dad is anti-dog because of allergies, so it would be super-cool to get a dog. Even if it's just for a few hours.

I can put up posters all around school and mention it on my blog and then all the students who want to participate will meet at Corner Park (which is so conveniently located on the corner by the school) this weekend and exchange their pet for someone else's. I will totally get an A for leadership and F-U-N!

The guidance counselor liked my idea a lot and said, "You could probably use some help with that, so why don't you and Lukas be co-leaders?"

As I nodded, I noticed out of the corner of my eye that Mia was staring. Actually, more like glaring at me with her jealous beady eyes. I couldn't help but smile inside.

RUMORS FROM THE BOYS' ROOM

I casually peeked around the corner from my locker and spotted Lukas talking excitedly with another boy. I didn't catch the whole conversation since I wasn't really eavesdropping or anything. And they might have been talking in low voices. But the conversation, from what I did hear, went something like this:

Lukas: So it's happening in two weeks? That's HUGE!

Other boy: Yep! He's a mastermind, for sure.

Lukas: . . . real lasers . . .

Other boy: . . . plan . . . evil!

Lukas: Wow! . . . the water?

Other boy: Whatever you do . . . don't . . . drink . . . because . . .

Lukas: . . . danger.

Wow is right! With details like these, I have to live up to my responsibility as the Blogtastic Blogger.

BREAKING NEWS FROM THE

BEST BLOG IN THE WORLD. EVER.

Students in the News: Alice is holding a reading contest with prizes for anyone who signs up for her new book club this month.

Mia St. Claire is accepting makeup donations for old people.

Sofia Becker is holding the APE program—Awesome Pet Exchange—at Corner Park this Saturday. Bring your pet to swap out for the afternoon! How fun, right?

Nona Bows is accepting an army of peaceful protesters tomorrow at lunch to boycott the cafeteria food.

School News: Something big will be happening in TWO WEEKS. All I can say is that it involves real lasers, a mastermind planner, and EVIL. Oh, and whatever you do, DON'T drink the water.

*Mr. A approved this post, so full names are allowed.

Blog Comment by Anon Student 1: Two weeks? I thought it was three?

Blog Comment by Anon Student 2: Yeah, I thought it was three weeks too. How did you get this inside info?

Blog Comment by Anon Student 3: Awesome! I've been waiting for Evil Mastermind 2!

Blog Comment by Anon Student 4: Another tip? I heard all the water is contaminated, even the rain! Thanks for the heads-up, Blogtastic!

In math class Mia St. Claire raises her hand all snobbishly and asks, "¿Puedo usar el baño?"

I hate when she asks things all fancy-like that I can't understand.

Is my outfit tan or ecru?

I don't think Ms. Peabody understands either, because she looks hypnotized by Mia's question. Mia, with a huge smile on her perfect face, leaves the classroom.

I do the only thing I can in a mysterious

situation such as this. I send my assistant to follow Mia and see what she's up to. And no, my assistant isn't Nona. Nona's my partner in crime. Even though we're completely crimeless.

As soon as Mia leaves the classroom, I elbow Alice and nod. She knows what has to be done. After all, we want the same thing:

TO. TAKE. MIA. DOWN.

As Alice gets up from her seat Ms. Peabody asks in a booming voice, "Where are you going?"

Alice did completely ignore the hand-raising rule, even though it was for a very good reason. She says, "To the bathroom." Then she does a dance, hopping from one foot to another. The grumpiness on Ms. Peabody's face disappears as she waves her hand for Alice to leave. I love when someone is able to think on her feet. Literally.

and dance

Nona pokes me in the back with the sharp end of her pencil, then leans forward to whisper in my ear.

"You know Mia went to the girls' room, right?"

I turn around in my seat and give my BFF a questioning look. "How do YOU know?"

"Baño is Spanish for bathroom."

"Again, how do YOU know?"

"Um, I take Spanish. With Mia. And your mom is our Spanish teacher."

Dumb. Who uses Spanish in math class? And obviously Ms. Peabody didn't know that. Or Alice. So take THAT, Nona! And who needs Spanish when you take French. Like me.

Mom keeps telling me I need to take Spanish. Guess what, Mom? Not gonna happen! I will take French until I practically become a . . . French person!

Mia returns to class looking all successfully Spanish-speaking. Her hair is all glimmering and shiny and extra-wavy. No doubt she went to the girls' room just to brush it like a trazillion times. Then I notice something different about her. Her lips are super-shiny too. It looks like . . . lip gloss. I look again, trying not to stare too obviously. Yes, I confirm, her lips _are_ in fact glossed.

Although I wish Mia's lips were zipped.

This can only mean one thing. She has a new plan of attack.

And on a totally different side note, Alice is still MIA. No, not Mia St. Claire, but Missing In Action (MIA for short).

But I would love it if Mia went MIA.

I figure there are three possibilities of what could've happened to Alice:

1. She fell in the toilet (this is why we always go in groups!).
2. She got sidetracked (happens to me all the time).
3. She got lost (happens to me never).

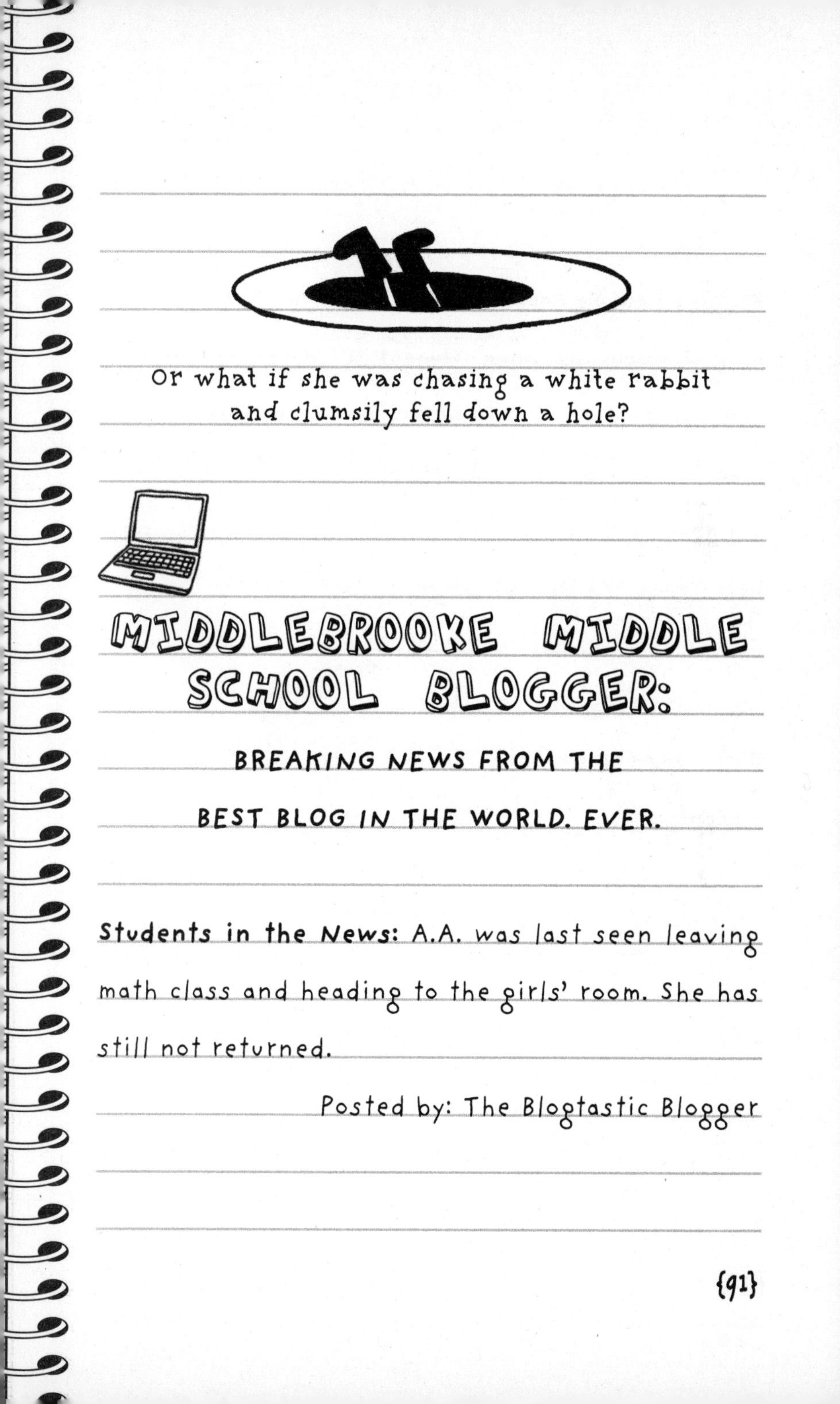

Or what if she was chasing a white rabbit and clumsily fell down a hole?

MIDDLEBROOKE MIDDLE SCHOOL BLOGGER:

BREAKING NEWS FROM THE BEST BLOG IN THE WORLD. EVER.

Students in the News: A.A. was last seen leaving math class and heading to the girls' room. She has still not returned.

Posted by: The Blogtastic Blogger

Blog Comment by Anon Student 1: Did anyone check the girls' room? Duh!

Blog Comment by Anon Student 2: Who's A.A.?

Blog Comment by Anon Student 3: Maybe the foreign exchange student? That would explain getting lost.

Blog Comment by Anon Student 4: Hey, knucklehead! Don't you know anything? The FES wouldn't go to the girls' room because the FES is a BOY! Named Lukas!

Blog Comment by Advisor Mr. A: Tone it down. Watch it with the name-calling and yelling.

Blog Comment by Anon Student 3: Why would a regular student get lost going to the girls' room?

Sunturday
12 & 13

AT CORNER PARK

I never realized how many students had foreign pets.

Types of foreign animals that resemble people I know

French poodle. Looks snooty like Penelope, right?

Siamese cat. All you need is a flower and POOF! Nona!

Australian gecko. It didn't really have a hat, but if it did, it would look just like Andrew!

Suddenly the thought of giving up my favorite pet ever puts a lump in my throat.

a lump the size of Mia St. Claire's bow

I still can't believe that Nona tried on three outfits before finally deciding what to wear today. She NEVER does that. She totally has a C-R-U-S-H.

Lukas helped me tag the pets with a number and then put the matching numbers in a bucket for each person to choose from, which would determine the pet they would end up with.

"Did you ever do stuff like this at your old school?" I asked him.

"No, we have clubs we join, though. My sister is in a dog-breeding club."

"What about you?"

"I play foosball."

I laughed. "You mean football."

"No. Foosball."

"Football."

"You know, where you kick the ball around."

"Oh. Soccer."

Lukas shrugged. "Yeah."

I made sure Sam Sam knew I was only exchanging him because I had to and that I would never, ever want to really trade him for another, more exciting pet. He seemed to understand.

I gave a list to Joey, the kid who got Sam Sam, about his likes (me) and dislikes (snooty people). I decided to educate Joey on the wonderfulness of my bird in case he overlooked the obviousness. And maybe I wanted to be a little show-offy about my smartness too.

Me: Parrots like Sam Sam are from the Amazon. That's in South America.

Joey (shrugs): My mom says birds are from Pet Barn.

He said BIRD, like Sam Sam is some ordinary everyday winged animal with feathers. And he's so not. He's a PARROT. A trainable animal that can talk and squawk and understand me AND my dislike for certain special, irritating individuals at school. And I won't name any names. MIA.

Math Cheater Megan (she cheated on a math test once and the name stuck) got a really gross rat that looked like it could hardly wait to climb out of its cage and attack her. What was she gonna do with that thing for a few hours?

Stand on a chair
and scream?

Bad news: I didn't get a dog.

More bad news: I ended up with a kitty-thing (I suppose it's really a kitty but it's so dirty it can only be called a thing).

Good news: Nona said it's Andrew's, so he will have to talk to me now!

At first (super-quick) glance, the kitty-thing looks like an adorable little fuzzy ball of cuteness. But on closer inspection, there's no cuteness or fuzz. Not even a speck of adorableness.

Kitty-thing is dirtier than dirt and his fur is super-messy and knotted, spiking out in all different directions. I know there must be eyes and a nose hidden in there somewhere.

And maybe a poodle?

There's only one reason why Andrew would have a kitty-thing:

He doesn't have time to wash it.

Boys like Andrew who are cute and funny (and so cute) and popular (and really cute) just don't have time for the normal everyday things like us non-populars. I mean, if I were super-popular (which I plan to be someday soon when my blog becomes popular) I wouldn't have much free time for ordinary things either.

Things I'd be busy doing if I were super-popular

I should probably add napping to my list. After all, being popular sounds pretty exhausting.

While brushing her fingers through her hair (since when does that happen?), Nona asks me what Lukas is going to do now that we all have our new pets.

Nona, who hardly ever gets angry (maybe only three times a week), punches me in the shoulder. "You don't have to be mean."

"Hey, Lukas!" I yell.

Nona turns to me. "Wait. Why are you calling him? What are you going to say? Tell me!"

She's still complain-whispering in my ear when I walk over to Lukas and ask him about his pet plans.

"We're taking the pets and going to Joey's house for a few minutes."

"Oh, well, make sure Joey is nice to the parrot.

That's my bird," I tell him in a total non-braggy voice.

"Yeah. Sure."

Lukas leaves and I realize how easy it is for boys. They don't have to do anything special, they just show up to a new school and suddenly have lots of friends. So now I know popularity is not only transferable, but also exchangeable.

AT HOME

Despite my mom being all teachery about our learning and doing our assignments like good kids, she refused to let kitty-thing come into the house.

Actually, her exact words were:

I WILL NOT LET THAT FILTHY CREATURE INTO THIS HOUSE!!!

When I pointed out that there was no need to be scared, it wasn't a creature, just a dirty little kitty-thing, she said:

OVER MY DEAD BODY!

Then she ran to the bathroom to throw up.

Dad said it's not Mom's fault she's behaving this way. It's the baby. Actually, he said it was the "pregnancy" but that's the same thing as blaming it on The Peanut. And how many times have Mom and Dad told me not to blame my bad actions on other people? And that other people can't MAKE me do something, I'm in control of myself and my own actions and blah blah blah?

Since Nona is thinking of getting a cat, I told her she really could use the practice so she can see what she's getting herself into and if she can handle the responsibility. So . . .

I make a warm bubbly bath.

Nona fails to understand how taking a bubble bath (especially since she'd taken a shower that morning) will help her take care of a kitty. Sigh. Isn't it obvious what I'm doing?

Nona rolls her eyes and says, "Everyone knows cats don't like baths. Besides, your mom said over her dead body."

I roll my eyes back at Nona. "If we sneak dirty kitty inside and give him a bath, then by the time Mom finds out, he'll be clean, so where's the problem?"

"Why do you care so much?" Nona asks.

It's not because it's Andrew's kitty.

We leave the bathroom for a minute to put my plan into action. Nona picks up kitty-thing with her special gloves (actually, they're Mom's dishwashing gloves) while I distract Dad long enough for her to bring him upstairs.

Nona brings him into the bathroom. The moment kitty-thing sees the tub, he has the tiniest bit of a reaction.

"Quick! Get him in the tub before he runs away!" I yell at Nona.

The next few moments are such a complete and horrible blur. I can barely remember all the specific details. But it went something like this:

1. A rocket shot out of the tub.
2. It started raining.
3. There was lots of noise.
4. And screaming (Nona).
5. A bright light flashed before my very eyes.
6. More screaming (me!).
7. Something big fell on top of us.

Now Nona and I are banned from using the bathroom anytime we're together in my house.

So. Not. Fair.

I asked Mom and Dad what if we really had to use the bathroom? Mom said to walk three doors down to Nona's house and let it be her mom's problem.

Mom said this when her face was very red and there was almost smoke coming from the top of her head. She held the sides of her pregnant (but small) belly like it gave her superpower strength. Or maybe more anger. I have a feeling The Peanut is already one huge anger ball transferring his or her unborn feelings onto my poor mom.

What would The Peanut have to be so angry about?

1. Can only eat what Mom eats (and that's a lot of gross adult food!).
2. Has to listen to Mom loudness all day.
3. And to Mom bronto-snores all night.
4. And feel "Dad pats" at random times while he's baby-talking to Mom's stomach.

For all we know, the "Dad pats" could be face spankings to the baby on the inside.

14

Blah. That's how the rest of the weekend was. Mainly because I didn't get to talk to Andrew. At all. He barely glanced in my direction when we were doing our pet exchange at the park.

It turns out kitty-thing WASN'T Andrew's cat!

I know, right? I even asked (demanded) how Nona could get such critical information incorrect.

Me: Why did you say kitty-thing was Andrew's, then?

Nona (shrugs): I saw him by the cat.

Me: By it? Geez, that's like something I would think. What's up with you?

Nona (shrugs): I was thinking about other things, I guess.

Me: Things like . . . Lukas?

Nona: Um, maybe.

Me: (sigh)

Also added to my list of Blah, the APE program didn't turn out the way it should have! The boys went over to Joey's house "for a few minutes" (actually the entire two hours!) and played video games! I have no idea what Sam Sam was doing that whole time. Actually, I do. He was listening to them play, because now he's repeating all these dumb video game phrases!

He says things like:

"Blow that up! Squawk!"

"Squawk! Wrong move, buddy!"

"Dude, look out! Squawk!"

Wait, what? Who's Amie? He must mean Sofia.

WHERE'S ALICE?

Nona and I decided to make posters to help find Alice and put them up if we still don't see her today. We did try finding her this weekend. Actually, we thought about it.

We thought about calling her cell. But we don't know the number.

We thought about visiting her. But we don't know where she lives.

Nona thinks her posters turned out way better than mine. I disagree and think mine are much more eye-catchingly creative.

IN THE HALL

I was on my way to gym, and Mom, who has break that period, was on her way to the teachers' lounge. And weirdest thing. Ever. She passed right by me and didn't even see me. She had this blank zombie-like look on her face.

Hey! Mom! It's me! Your student-daughter!

Mom turned around and raised her arm in a limp wave. She looked so tired. I felt really bad. Then I felt super-bad when I realized I'd just had a mom moment. Yes, for that moment, I had turned into my mom!

ZOMBIE CLASS

While everyone is reading quietly from their books and the room is practically silent (most probably due to a bad case of Zombiness), I decide to show Mia she's not the only one who can be all super-show-offy with her language skills. So I raise my hand in a non-snobbish-but-I-mean-serious-business way.

But the teacher is reading too and doesn't see me. So I clear my throat loudly.

"Ahem!"

Okay, maybe not loudly enough because still nobody notices me.

So then I say, "Excusez-moi!" super-loudly.

Every head in the class snaps up to look in my direction, including the teacher's. And Mia's.

I smile.

Mr. Allen doesn't look at me all hypnotic, though—more like annoyed. Finally he points his pencil at me and says, "Yes?"

My brain gets stage fright as I search for the French translation for "girls' room."

"Restroom?" he asks.

Yes! I want to shout, but I think quickly on my feet and yell out the French word for yes.

Which is pronounced "wee, wee."

The whole class bursts out laughing. Including the teacher! And what's worse, I hear Nona snickering behind me.

"No!" I yell. "I mean loo." Okay, so it's not French, but it's the British word for bathroom. And if nothing else, it shows my multicultural progression in the last 43½ hours.

"What? What did you say about me?"

I turn around to see an angry look on Lou's face. Oh no, he thought I was talking about HIM?

What?
You think I
stink like
a bathroom?

RUMORS FROM THE BOYS' ROOM

Zach committed fraud on his English test. He was actually bragging to his buddies about how he "scored an A" and was glad he sat next to Alexander because if Alexander wasn't so smart Zach might have failed his English test.

THE RETURN OF LOST ALICE

Alice is back!

After class, Lost Alice tells us her story of not

being lost, just sick. But still, that's how nicknames happen.

Nicknaming history at Middlebrooke

Spiderman.
Because Jeremy collects spiders.

Ninja Girl.
Every time Jessica walks by, she waves and says hi like a ninja.

Lost Alice: I was right behind Mia in the girls' room. Practically inches behind her.

Me: When you follow someone, you don't actually let them see you following them.

Lost Alice (rolls eyes): Anyway, she was spraying all this shiny spritz stuff in her hair, but like way too much of it, and she sprayed it all over me. On purpose too, I think. I had to go to the nurse's office after that because I thought I had been sprayed to death. But luckily, I ended up going home and recovering.

SIGH.

For a moment there, when she rolled her eyes, she scarily resembled Mia St. Claire.

My and Nona's eyes light up like . . . well, like whatever lights up really bright, because this is big. No, this is bigger than big. This is massively monstrous! Nona looks at Lost Alice, staring her down. "Well?" she asks.

"Well what?"

Nona shakes her head. She's very impatient with . . . well, just about everything. "Tell us Mia's secrets."

"She uses a hair spritz made of only water and salt. Sea salt." She whispers the secret ingredient.

I shrug. "I don't get it. What does that do?"

Lost Alice looks at me all wide-eyed like I just asked her when the world is going to end. "It makes your hair wavy. Naturally."

"Oh." Hmm, that gives me an idea.

AFTER SCHOOL

I tested out the sea-salt hair-spritz theory.

I think Mia might realize
I stole her hair secret,
so I probably won't
actually wear
my hair like this.

Nona is holding another peaceful protest today since not many people showed up last time.

Actually, it was just me and her.

So this time she thought bribery would help and handed out candy bars to everyone who agreed not to buy the cafeteria food and instead promised to spend their lunchtime holding a picket sign. I guess it worked, because the lunch lady called Nona over and asked for her list of demands.

But then it didn't work out, because the lunch

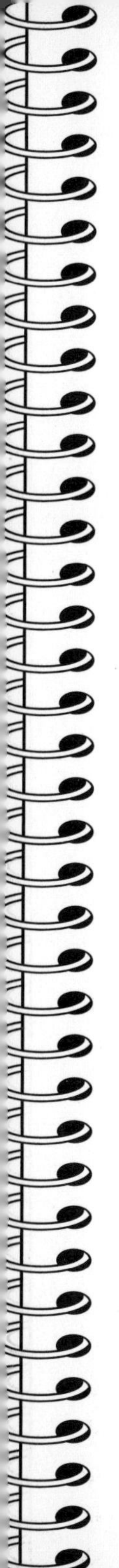

lady looked at the list and laughed at her. Then she said, "What do I look like, a chef?"

DEMANDS
No more meat loaf
PIZZA BUFFET
soda fountain
FResh Smoothies (instead of fresh fruit)
mandatory dessert

And she was only giving up for a few minutes.

Nona said she refuses to give up, though.

But then Lukas walked into the cafeteria and Nona went over to talk to him.

When she came back, she said she'd think of a compromise with the lunch lady.

RUMORS FROM THE BOYS' ROOM

There was a huge fight by the boys' room today! One boy had a kid in a headlock and another boy was twisted like a pretzel. They were grunting and breathing hard. Three other boys were cheering. And Lukas was there too. He wasn't part of the fight, though, just an excited observer. Like me!

MIDDLEBROOKE MIDDLE SCHOOL BLOGGER:

BREAKING NEWS FROM THE BEST BLOG IN THE WORLD. EVER.

Students in the News: A huge fight broke out today outside the boys' room. One boy even had another in a headlock. No idea who it was, because I'm totally not a gossiper.

Blog Comment by Advisor Mr. A: We do not tolerate violence on school grounds. We will look into this.

WEDNESDAY

16

MORNING MOM WEIRDNESS

Mom talked to her stomach this morning on the drive to school. And not just talked, but tried to get her stomach to take sides against me! The creepiness of the conversation went something like this:

Mom: We should drive to school every day.

Me: I like riding my bike with my friends.

Mom (talking to stomach): But it's nice spending family time together, isn't it, Peanut?

Me (ignoring The Peanut): We spend family time at home.

Mom (talking to stomach): But the morning is nice too, don't you agree with me? Yeah, I think Sofia is being stubborn too.

I gave up and let her have her talk with The Peanut.

AT LUNCH . . .

I invited Lukas to sit with us at lunch but he'd already been invited to sit with Mia and Maddie. I could tell Nona was angry, even though she said she wasn't.

So I gave her some girly advice. I told her she should borrow one of my cute shirts and wear her hair down. You know, dress a little bit girlier. At first I thought she was going to throw her orange at my head. But then she seemed to have second thoughts and she put her orange down and said, "You know, you might be right."

Whoa! Where did Nona go? I just smiled and nodded and went with it. Who am I to argue? Of course, I'm sure it didn't hurt that Alice was there nodding the whole time too.

WHY LUNCH TURNED MORE HORRIBLE

Could it be true that MY Andrew is totally oblivious to an act of sheer stupidity starring Mia St. Claire? Because at lunch today, Mia made a point of sitting next to him and Andrew made a point of NOT scooting away. Like to the other side of the room.

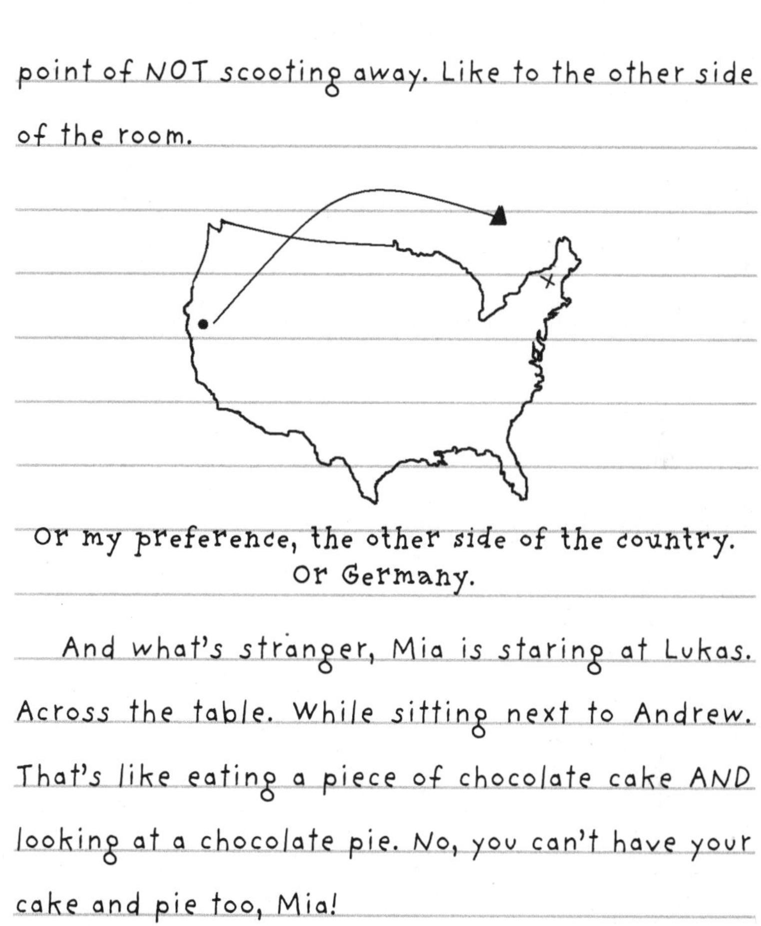

Or my preference, the other side of the country. Or Germany.

And what's stranger, Mia is staring at Lukas. Across the table. While sitting next to Andrew. That's like eating a piece of chocolate cake AND looking at a chocolate pie. No, you can't have your cake and pie too, Mia!

Nona is happily chomping on her orange, peel and all. Why must I be the only one suffering?

Me: Nona! Mia is eyeballing <u>your</u> Lukas!

Nona: And she's sitting next to your Andrew.

Me: While she's hypnotically looking at your Lukas.

Nona: At least my Lukas can turn her to stone, right? What can your Andrew do?

Me: You're so mean.

Nona (smiles): I know. But Lukas winked at me earlier!

There should be a rule against fake winking!

RUMORS FROM THE BOYS' ROOM

Long-Legged Lenny is said to have tried out for the basketball team but didn't make it. Some boy named Junior told Lou that he can dunk Oreos better than Lenny can dunk basketballs!

THURSDAY 17

Alice shared some more of Mia's super secrets today. But nothing compares to her last secret, which was that in her bag Mia keeps a bunch of lip gloss, probably in a variety of flavors, that she has expensively shipped over from faraway lands just for her.

Alice said there was a lot of sparkly and glittery stuff in there, too much to figure out what exactly. But we already know it's that stuff that makes her eyes shine and her teeth sparkle and her hair glimmer and—gag! Whatever. What was the point of all this again?

So Alice tried to duplicate some of this glittery and flavorful stuff (she raided her mom's makeup bag) and we tried it out on Nona. We also took her glasses off and gave her a different hairstyle.

Nona looked fabulous! Minus the part where she couldn't see anything without her glasses. So we gave those back to her. When she was finally able to see herself in the mirror, her reaction was different from what we were expecting.

I told her to trust me. Alice nodded. Lukas would totally fall head over heels for her now.

We did get her to agree to try the new look at school, though, by telling her to think of it as an experiment. And we might also have bribed her too.

RUMORS FROM THE BOYS' ROOM

OMG! I just heard that the boys who were fighting on Tuesday were finally discovered and are now in the principal's office. They are so busted! But then someone else said it was the Blogtastic Blogger's fault! I blogged the truth; it's not my fault those boys decided to break school rules. Then someone else said the Blogtastic Blogger would get it!

MORE MOM STRANGENESS

Mom is now suffering from heartburn. She says drinking milk helps but drinking water makes it worse.

Maybe someone should alert
the fire department?

18

WHAT HAVE YOU DONE?

Those are the first words Nona says to me as soon as I see her. Then she pulls me over to her locker and tells me the news more quietly.

Nona: The Blogtastic Blogger is losing all of "her" readers.

Me: What? Why?

Nona: How can the Blogtastic Blogger be so clueless to everything else going around? Don't you read the other blogs?

Me: Shhh! Someone might hear. And

no, there aren't any worth reading.

Nona: Well, now there is.

Nona takes me to the library, stating it's a computer emergency. She pulls up the school blogs and clicks on Max's, aka Bloghead boy's.

MIDDLEBROOKE MIDDLE SCHOOL BLOGGER:

REAL INFORMATION, NOT THE MADE-UP STUFF.

To all the cool people who read my blog: The Blogtastic Blogger has struck again. Not only has she given you wrong information many times, but now she's trying to sabotage my blog and my friends. And maybe Blogtastic isn't even a girl, but someone pretending to be a girl. All I know is this person almost had me and my friends suspended! And it was for nothing! It was because we were talking about the newest wrestling game outside the boys' room. And so what if we were giving each other wrestling tips? That means we were fighting? The Blogtastic Blogger is a troublemaker and, since she can't handle a little blog competition, is trying to get us suspended.

And why do you need to read that blog for gaming advice anyway? C.C.'s blog, Gamers Addiction, has every game with every tip you can imagine!

Posted by: Max Magee, The Bloghead Blogger

Nona: Where are you getting all this bloggy info you're posting?

Look! I have Chocolate!

I quickly distract Nona from the question.

Nona and I are THIS close to telling Alice about my secret identity as the Blogtastic Blogger. We figure an extra pair of ears could help us for sure. Besides, we know we can totally trust Alice with our secret.

We were thinking of maybe telling her this weekend, but Mom had a surprise for me, so we put the idea on hold.

Dad was at home painting the soon-to-be Peanut's room some shade of pastel, so it was a day for me and Mom. Just the two of us (two and a half if you count The Peanut).

Mom was so excited to get her toenails painted. She said she's wanted to paint them for a while, but she can't even see her feet, let alone touch them.

Mom: You know, my belly was much bigger than this even when I was pregnant with you.

Me: How big?

Mom: I had to roll off the couch just to stand up.

I'm glad I wasn't drinking anything, because I would've totally snorted it up my nose.

Me: At least I didn't make you snore!

Mom: What are you talking about? I don't snore!

Me: Ha! Maybe I should record you.

And then Mom totally surprised me when she said she wanted me to help her name the baby.

I couldn't help but feel excited. Just a teeny tiny bit, though.

Okay, so Mom doesn't want to know if the baby will be a boy or a girl before it's born (she thinks surprises are great. Whatever). But I guess we can think of the best names for both. I agreed to help with naming. I mean, if I don't step in to help, The Peanut is likely to be named after a piece of furniture. And all the good furniture names are already taken.

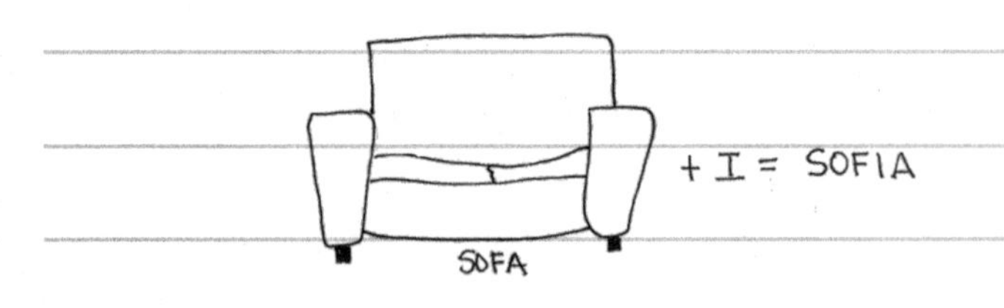

AT HOME

After we got back from our girls' day, Mom and I went up to the attic, where she pulled out a box and said, "Guess what this is?"

"I have no idea. Something old and dusty?"

She smiled as she took out a tiny pink dress.

"I thought you didn't want to know if it would be a boy or girl yet," I said.

"This, Sofia, used to be your dress."

I was really THAT small?

Mom nodded. "And if the baby is a girl, what do you think about her wearing your old dress?"

"That would be cool! And if it's a boy, he

probably wouldn't care that he's wearing pink. Or a dress."

"I'm just kidding, Mom!"

Lately Mom's been really emotional, so I think it's harder for her to tell if I'm joking. But really, my jokes are so funny, how could someone not know?

Other moments of emotional Mom

I can't believe Mom saved something for so long. And to think The Peanut might wear a dress I wore when I was a baby? How weirdly cool!

MONDAY 21

NAME THE BABY

As soon as I tell Alice and Nona that I get to help come up with names for The Peanut, they instantly begin yelling suggestions at me.

I guess the expression on my face is enough to make them realize how serious I really am. So they start yelling out other names.

Why are they so excited? And why are they thinking of names that are way cooler than mine?

I stomp away to my locker, determined to be the best big sister ever and the one who comes up with the perfect baby name. In the meantime, I hope to catch some news from the boys' room that could help bring me into a happier mood.

RUMORS FROM THE BOYS' ROOM

Whose idea was it to listen to these boys? Besides hearing unreliable info, I'm also forced to hear something horrible. Terrible. Absolutely the worst! Andrew happened to be in the boys' room and I just happened to have my ear pressed close to the wall.

He was talking about a girl! Not me. Or Mia. Or

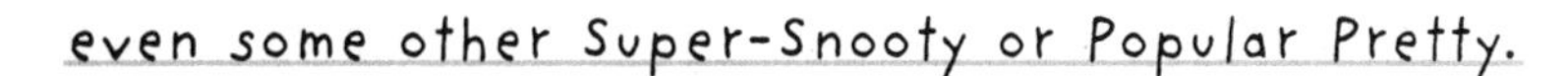

even some other Super-Snooty or Popular Pretty.

It was worse than that.

It was an unknown.

Her name is Amie. That's what Sam Sam had told me too. But I really thought he overheard wrong. Or spoke wrong. It happens.

Andrew said he misses her. And he mentioned how much she loves watching TV with him. (Hello! I love watching TV too!) So of course a bazillion questions stampede through my mind like a group of elephants on a safari hunt.

And then I do the only thing I can at precisely that exact moment.

I pout.

RUMORS FROM THE BOYS' ROOM

Lukas said he's never kissed a girl! Well, it's not really a big deal or anything, but then Joey said he's kissed two girls! I wonder who?

Or maybe he kissed one girl twice?

IN MATH CLASS

When I see Lukas, I ask him about his sister. You know, in case she has a totally cool name that I could suggest to Mom.

"You said you have a sister, right?"

"One older sister," he said.

"What's her name?"

"Kadja."

Hmm, don't think I'll suggest that one. Especially since I can't pronounce it.

AFTER SCHOOL

Nona, Alice, and I are trying to get more information out of Sam Sam. Spending time at Joey's house with the other boys turns out to have been not such a bad thing after all. It's like Sam Sam was a super-secret bird spy.

"Does Andrew like Mia?" I ask Sam Sam.

"Take Mia down. Squawk!"

Nona and I look at each other and shrug.

"Can you say Joey?" asks Alice.

Sam Sam repeats back the same sentence to Alice.

"Your turn," I say to Nona.

She thinks a minute before saying, "Lukas."

"Lukas, six toes. Squawk!"

We laugh so hard and Nona's face turns so red.

"I'm sure Sam Sam is wrong."

"Mia is pretty. Squawk!"

"See," I tell them. "He's so wrong!"

Parrots are very unreliable.

BUT . . . what if Sam Sam repeated certain things while he was at Joey's house?

WEDNESDAY

23

ALICE WONDERS

Alice really should keep her wondering to herself instead of talking out loud (very loud) in the hallways. With tons of students around. All it does is cause contagiousness. Luckily, I have Nona, who always saves the day.

Alice (looking directly at me): I wonder how the Blogtastic Blogger knows everything?

Me: No idea.

Alice: But don't you ever wonder?

Me: Not really.

Lukas: I wonder. I hear about her all the time. Where do I read her blog?

Alice: Oh, I can tell you about it.

Me: Don't waste his time.

Lukas: It's not a waste.

Nona: It's uncool to read blogs.

Nona is dressed all pretty again but I notice that Lukas hasn't said anything to her about her makeover. He's probably shy. I guess he's so shy that he doesn't really talk to her now that he sits by her in class either. Boys are just weird like that. It took me forever to get Andrew to notice me.

Other ways I tried to get Andrew to notice me

I said hi to him. From a distance.

But the fact that Andrew gave me a pet name is HUGE. Even if it is Barfia. I've never heard him call Mia by any other name.

I could give him some suggestions, such as . . .

MIA TORTILLA

OR . . .

That girl who likes to steal all the other girls' crushes.

Hmm . . . I wonder if he has a nickname for this Amie girl.

RUMORS FROM THE BOYS' ROOM

I almost got caught! I glimpsed something pretty terrible when I was NOT spying on the boys' room. Jimmy Turler was wearing his super-baggy pants again and his boxers were showing! Worst part? They were SpongeBob boxers! I snorted so loud everyone looked in my direction. But I hid quickly around the wall, being super-discreet. I don't think anyone saw me, but I do think it was enough to distract them from the bright yellowness of Jimmy's boxers. Not intentional.

MIDDLEBROOKE MIDDLE SCHOOL BLOGGER:

BREAKING NEWS FROM THE

BEST BLOG IN THE WORLD. EVER.

Students in the News: M.M., J.S., and T.L. were the ones outside the boys' room fighting. They got only one day of detention each because they claimed to be fake-fighting and were only practicing wrestling moves on each other.

Posted by: The Blogtastic Blogger

THURSDAY 24

MORNING MOM WEIRDNESS

This morning, Mom was being dramatic and picky. Like she insisted we drive with ALL the windows down. Because she was so hot even though it was like 50 degrees outside. But two seconds later she said she was freezing and rolled all the windows up. As soon as she did, she said she was suffocating. So back down with the windows.

MY MIND IS MADE UP.

Sort of. I need a way to redeem my blog and fight against that nonsense boy blogger who thinks he knows everything but in fact knows absolutely nothing.

Ideas for blog posts:

1. Interview someone worth reading about (need a way to interview anon).
2. Do a pathetic, groveling apology post (use as last resort).
3. Make up something mean about that Bloghead and give him a taste of his own medicine.

the super-gross medicine that makes you gag just by looking at it

AT LUNCH

A quiet protest led by Nona ended with another list of demands. This time the lunch lady laughed at her and said, "Show me the money."

Apparently it's not in the school budget to serve really good food.

RUMORS FROM THE BOYS' ROOM

Jason hasn't showered in a week! Max Magee (the dumb Bloghead boy) dared him to not take a shower and now all the boys are taking bets on how long he will go. I think I could smell him all the way from my locker! Glad I don't have classes with him.

AFTER SCHOOL

Nona agreed with me that I should post an interview on my blog. But we would have to interview someone that all the popular kids would want to read about, which would then make everyone else want to read. So we put ourselves in Mia's shoes. Who would Mia want to read about the most?

Herself!

So we decided to interview Miss Popular Pretty (gag!) because we know she would want everyone and their cats to read our blog so they could see how wonderful she thinks she is. The plan is foolproof! We get back our readers and Mia is . . . well, still Mia.

The main problem is thinking of a way to get the questions to her and back, while being super-secretly discreet. My lightbulb flashes and then . . . I got it! We'll drop the questions through the slots of Mia's locker with instructions to leave the answers with Mr. A. He won't tell our secret. He can't. He's a teacher and teachers can't tell secrets about their students, right? Then we'll send Alice in to get the answers back from Mr. A. And maybe we'll have her read them with us, and she'll finally know I'm the Blogtastic Blogger!

MIDDLEBROOKE MIDDLE SCHOOL BLOGGER:

BREAKING NEWS FROM THE

BEST BLOG IN THE WORLD. EVER.

Animals in the News: N.B. has lost a lost dog. The dog's name is Barney, although he doesn't have tags. He is wearing a blue beaded necklace around his neck, though, which belongs to N.B. Please comment if found.

Posted by: The Blogtastic Blogger

25

RUMORS FROM THE BOYS' ROOM

Lukas came out of the boys' room with a wet paper towel pressed against his forehead. Apparently, he has a huge zit! It looks like a gigantic pink gumball. But the other boys are laughing because he called it a "pickle." Nona looked it up and that just means a pimple in German.

What is it with these countries and food? And why a pickle?

If Mia had a zit, she would probably call it something fancy, like a soufflé.

64 MINUTES, 31 SECONDS LATER

Lukas finds me before zombie class and says I can have my seat back next to Nona.

Me: I thought you liked Nona.

Lukas: She's nice.

Me: And haven't you noticed how girly and pretty she's been?

Lukas: Yeah, I've noticed.

Me: (sigh)

Why are boys so complicated? It's obvious Mia has overtaken him. He should just admit it.

Of course I switch my seat back. But Nona doesn't even notice. Or at least, she pretends not to. She acts like I was there the entire time. Maybe she doesn't like Lukas anymore? Or maybe it's the pickle pimple.

UPDATE: PROJECT LEADERSHIP

Our guidance counselor asked how we're doing on our projects and some of the students gave an update or showed photos. We're supposed to write a five-page paper and include photos by the end of the month.

Mia's project: makeovers for old people.

Nona shared with the class that her project has been a flop. The lunch lady has laughed at her more

My homeless clients were satisfied with their clothing but didn't even know what Gucci, Louis Vuitton, or Prada was. I'm very disappointed.

Penelope's project:
designer clothing drive for homeless

times than she can count on her fingers and toes and the only thing she was able to have changed on the menu was that one piece of fresh fruit was added daily.

The guidance counselor said Nona didn't flop, she did exactly what she set out to do. She took a lead role, and even if you can't always change everything at once, making a small change is a very good start. Nona probably couldn't have made all those changes herself anyway; the school board would need to be involved.

26 & 27

Alice and Nona came over on Saturday and we helped Mom and Dad with the baby's room.

Actually, the office was changed into The Peanut's room. At least I don't have to share mine.

Dad painted the walls a pale green and put up borders of baby BaZooples. They look like cute normal animals so I have no idea what BaZoople actually means.

Who knew folding a trillion tiny baby clothes would be so tiring?

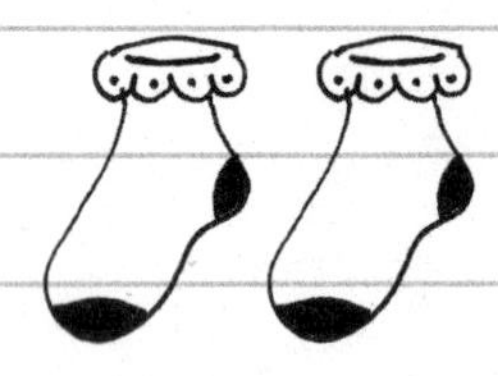

And why does a baby
need thousands of baby socks?
It's not like it can walk
and get them dirty or something.

Mom had to take a nap right away, so she put me in charge. It was fun picking out which sheets to put on the crib and deciding where everything should go.

Alice and Nona stayed for dinner and I wish they hadn't. You would think we'd have gotten used to the mom weirdness, but it's so random and unexplainable.

Mom made us dinner. Spaghetti.

We all sat down to eat and Mom said, "Ewww! This is so gross!" Which was so weird because she made it.

Mom dangled the noodles off her fork and said, "This looks like worms." We all looked to Dad

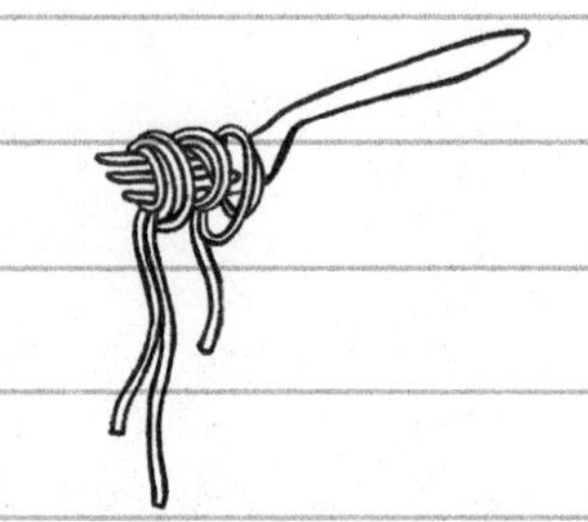

for his reaction, mainly to see if it was okay to laugh, but he just stared at her too.

Mom did the whole stomach-talking thing like she had in the car and said, "We don't like this gross food, do we, Peanut?" She got up from the table and announced that "they" decided they were going out for ice cream, then left by herself.

I think it's started already, just like people said it would. The Peanut is getting special treatment over me, and it's only a bump in Mom's stomach. Sigh.

I rode with Mom to school this morning. On purpose. But only because I wanted to get there earlier than usual and talk to Nona as soon as she arrived. Especially since she wasn't calling me back.

It seemed like Mom was almost normal, until she started complaining about me.

Mom (wrinkles nose): Your breath stinks. It smells like . . . mint.

Me: My toothpaste is minty.

Mom: Don't use so much next time.

Me: I really didn't use _that_ much.

Mom: It smells like you used the whole tube.

Then she rolled down all the windows. Until four seconds later when she said she was freezing and rolled them back up. And then the minty freshness of my breath was just too overwhelming again, windows back down.

I CAN'T BELIEVE MY EYES.

I endured all the Mom nightmarishness and froze my butt off and Nona still got to school before me. Not only is she looking all normal and non-girly, but she's not by herself. Lukas is hanging out at her locker.

I stomp right up to them and casually mention that Nona's "handy" is most probably broken on account of her not calling me back.

All she says is sorry. She was busy. Busy playing video games the rest of the weekend with Lukas! She must've also been too busy to do her hair and pick out cutesy, girly clothes too.

My brain numbness kicks in at precisely that exact moment, because I have absolutely nothing to say.

AT LUNCH

While Nona is in the girls' room, I catch up to Lukas and ask him the one question on my mind. I can't resist. I HAVE to know.

Me: Why do you like Nona now when you didn't before?

Lukas: She's fun again.

Me: What do you mean . . . again?

Lukas: I liked her because she wasn't like all those other girls.

But then she turned into one of them.

Me: Turned into one of them?

Lukas: Yes. Dressing like them, wearing her hair like them. That's just fade.

Me: Um, fade?

Lukas: You know. Like classes you want to fall asleep in because they're so fade. Same thing.

Me: I think you mean boring. And Nona is never boring. Even if she dressed all girly, she was still the same Nona.

Lukas: Not really. She's much more fun being the way she was. I really like her now.

Boys are so weird! I had an excellent idea,

though. I told Lukas he should get Nona something, like a new flower for her hair. A small gift.

Why would I want to kill her?

Who knew that in Germany "gift" means poison?

Then I suggested he should get Mia a gift.

Speaking of Mia, we folded the questions for the blog interview and secretly placed them in the slots of her locker. Actually, Nona did. She left class pretending she was going to the girls' room.

RUMORS FROM THE BOYS' ROOM

Christian Dean was bragging today. Actually, he brags a lot. But still. Today I just happened to overhear him bragging about acing a surprise quiz in pre-algebra. Normally, it wouldn't be braggy to talk about a good grade, but he was all like, "I aced the test! Take that! In your face! Did any of you get a 100% like me? I barely had to study. I hardly ever do. I just naturally get As on everything."

NEWS!

Mom wasn't feeling good and left school early. She never leaves early!

So I'm getting a ride home with Alice and her dad. But guess who gets into the car with us?

Okay, somebody got into the wrong car!

And then Mia . . . she said the most absurd thing. Ever. She said to Alice's dad:

Hey, Uncle James!

Uh, WHAT?

I sat in the front seat while Alice, Mia, and Maddie were in the back. It smelled like a whole fruit stand with all the hair flinging going on.

And then Mia whispered something and Maddie laughed (of course), but so did Alice! There is something terribly, horribly wrong here.

How did Nona and I NOT know that Alice and Mia are related? This calls for answers, so I quickly wrote up a blog post. With a poll, naturally. And the good thing about polls is that full names can be used. As long as everything is factually right, of course.

MIDDLEBROOKE MIDDLE SCHOOL BLOGGER:

BREAKING NEWS FROM THE

BEST BLOG IN THE WORLD. EVER.

How many of you realize that certain people in this school are related? Posted below is a poll.

BLOG POLL
(click if you know)

- Sofia's mom is Spanish teacher Mrs. Becker.
- Penelope's brother is some boy in 8th grade.
- Mia and Alice are cousins.
- Bethany and Emily are twins. Fraternal.

TUESDAY 29

Mom still isn't feeling good, so no school again. I volunteered to stay home with her, but she rejected my clever idea.

Nona rocks! She had a terrific idea after I told her last night that Alice and Mia are—gulp—cousins. But first, the Blogtastic poll results so far:

BLOG POLL RESULTS

100% knew about Sofia's mom
12% knew about Penelope's brother
90% knew about Mia and Alice
98% knew about the twins

Poll percents. Not many people knew about Penelope's brother, but a lot of students will know about Mia and Alice.

So how are Nona and I so clueless? I've known Mia for way too many years.

NONA'S IDEA

Nona decided to talk to Lukas today. About Alice. Since he's living with Mia he can tell us if Alice visits Mia a lot and if they are secretly good friends and Alice has just been lying to us.

RUMORS FROM THE BOYS' ROOM

I heard Matthew Rushing talking to himself by the boys' room. He was asking himself why nobody talks to him. Then he answered himself.

ALICE SAYS . . .

Alice is hard to ignore. She kept getting right up in my face until I would talk to her.

"We're just cousins, not friends. What's the big deal?"

Uh, being related to the worst girl ever is a HUGE deal!

And then Alice says, "Besides, it's not like we're blood related or anything. Her mom married into our family."

That would explain why Nona and I didn't know about her before.

But it's still a big deal.

And maybe an even bigger deal is that Nona and I seem to be at the very bottom of the information chain. Very bottom.

FROM LUKAS'S MOUTH

So Lukas told Nona that he didn't ever see Alice at Mia's. Which either means that they really aren't friends or that Alice is really good at backstabbing. I don't know about that, but Nona says we'd be stupid to pick up the interview notes from Mr. A or send Alice to get them. She knows too much and can't be trusted. I guess it would be way too risky picking up the notes ourselves and we can't trust anyone else. Oh well. At least we didn't tell Alice about my secret identity like Nona was insisting.

AT HOME

I can barely believe my eyes! I forgot all about looking at comments on the post about Nona's dog, Barney. It seems the news about the lost dog was a hit! People are actually leaving comments for him. And the biggest surprise—someone found a dog down the street with a blue beaded necklace around his neck. Barney!

I'm not going to say it, but I knew I was right!

A few other students left comments asking if they could be interviewed on the blog, and one girl even said she lost her cat and wanted to know if the Blogtastic Blogger could help her. Maybe getting other students involved with the blog will make it even more popular! See, we didn't even need that dumb interview with Mia.

I would've had to gag while posting that blog entry too.

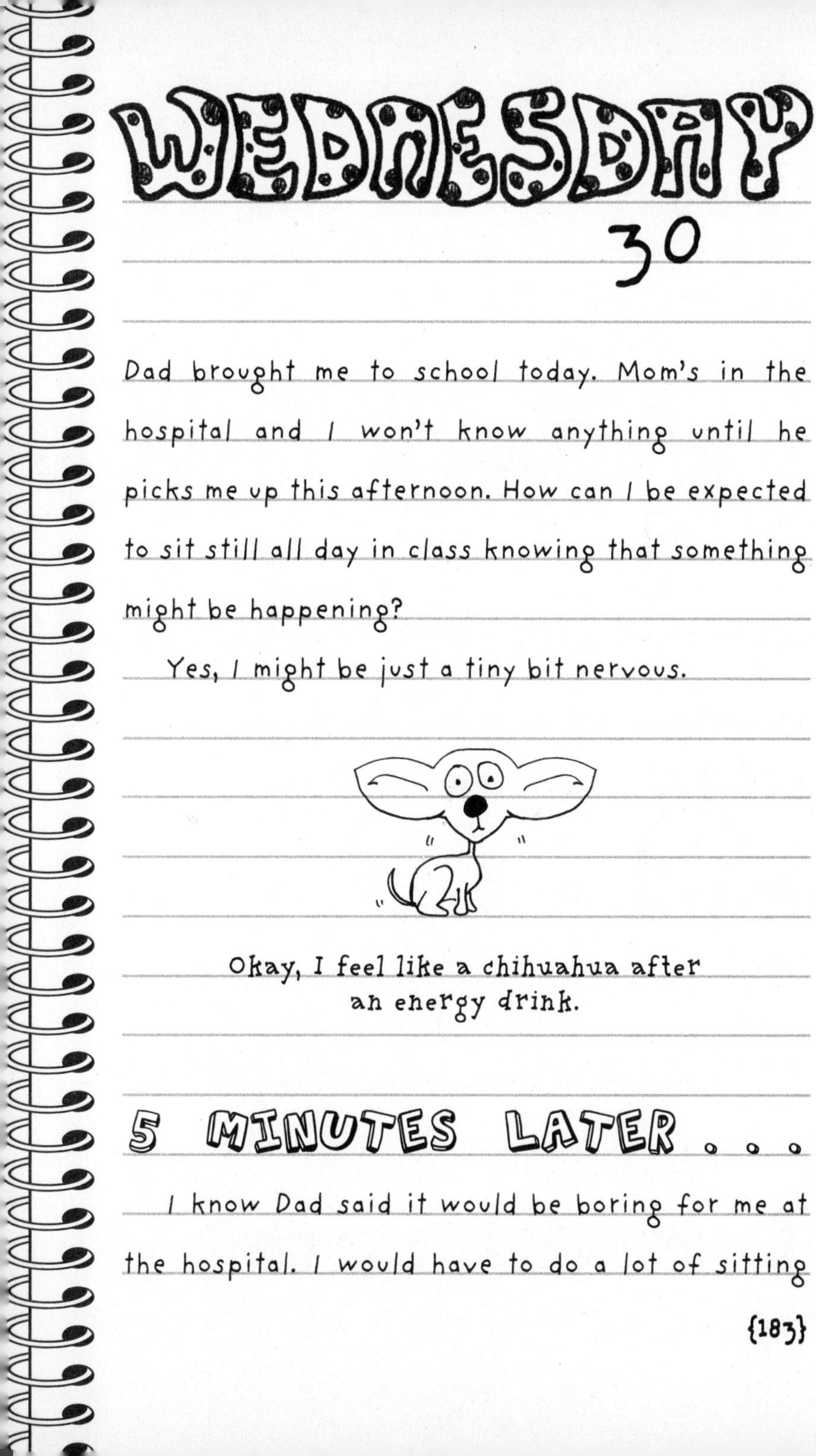

WEDNESDAY 30

Dad brought me to school today. Mom's in the hospital and I won't know anything until he picks me up this afternoon. How can I be expected to sit still all day in class knowing that something might be happening?

Yes, I might be just a tiny bit nervous.

Okay, I feel like a chihuahua after an energy drink.

5 MINUTES LATER . . .

I know Dad said it would be boring for me at the hospital. I would have to do a lot of sitting around and waiting. But doesn't he realize how boring it is for me at school? I'm doing just a lot of sitting and waiting here too.

2-1/2 MINUTES LATER . . .

Oh no! Found out that Barney's real owner is also a Middlebrooke student. It's Andrew!

Super-good news, though: that means Andrew reads MY blog! But on a non-selfish note, I'm sad that Nona lost Barney. Again.

6 MINUTES LATER . . .

Ooh! I caught Nona and Lukas holding hands. But when they saw me, they totally denied it. Lukas is going back home to Germany next week, so I'll wait till he's gone to tease Nona.

3 MINUTES LATER . . .

I can't take this waiting anymore. I just might go crazy. And why is TGBE drooling on his desk? Does he not remember how to close his mouth? Yuck!

7-3/4 MINUTES LATER . . .

Why does time always go by slower when you're waiting for something? Maybe I'll pretend not to wait.

30 SECONDS LATER . . .

Nope. Doesn't work. Sigh.

Time is going by soooo slow. Slower than trying to Rollerblade on sand.

SCHOOL IS OUT!!!

Dad is parked right out front waiting for me. As I walk quickly to the car, I stop in mid-step as

I hear my name being called. But not just my name. My *pet* name. And it's the sweetest sound I've ever heard in my entire life.

Hey, Barfia!

Just having Andrew near me makes my heart melt.

like two scoops of chocolate fudge ice cream in a waffle cone in the middle of the Sahara Desert

Andrew is holding out a paper. "You dropped this, Barfia."

Under normal circumstances I would stare at him for at least five minutes longer, but I grab the paper, mutter thanks, and head to Dad's car.

Did I really just blow Andrew off?

No time to worry about that now.

As soon as I jump into the car, I ask Dad, "Well?"

He only shakes his head and smiles. "We'll be there in a few and you'll see."

I get a gut-wrenching feeling and I'm not sure if it's dread or the slightest bit of excitement.

31

No school today! Well, just not for me. But I managed to take a few minutes to update my blog!

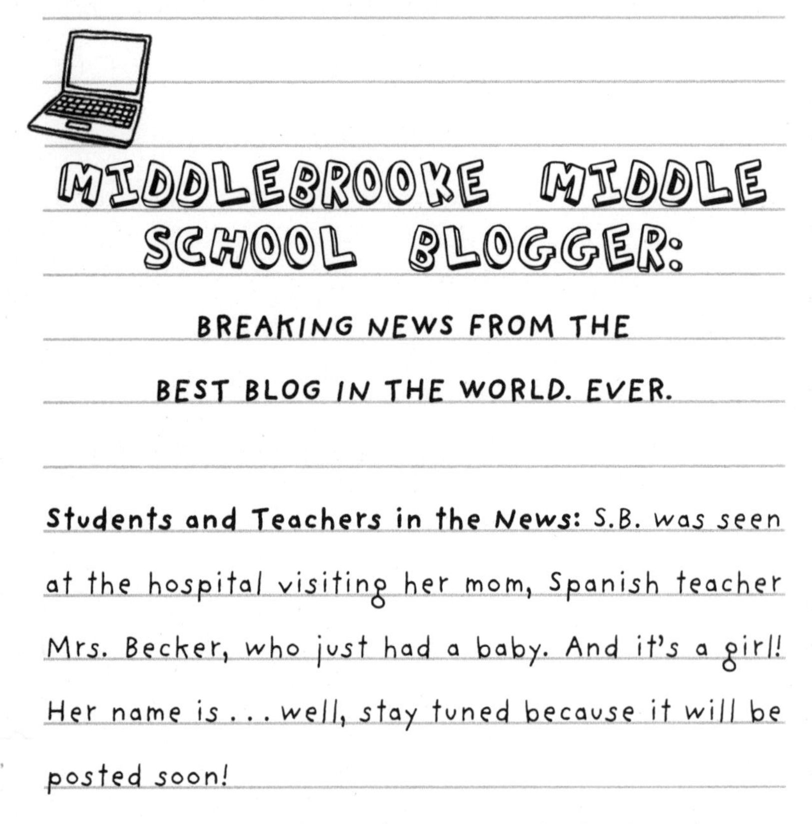

MIDDLEBROOKE MIDDLE SCHOOL BLOGGER:

BREAKING NEWS FROM THE BEST BLOG IN THE WORLD. EVER.

Students and Teachers in the News: S.B. was seen at the hospital visiting her mom, Spanish teacher Mrs. Becker, who just had a baby. And it's a girl! Her name is . . . well, stay tuned because it will be posted soon!

Posted by: The Blogtastic Blogger

Okay, so I couldn't post too much about The Peanut because then it might seem a little suspicious and I wouldn't be anon anymore. My new baby sister, Halli, is super-adorable. SUPER! She is so tiny I can hold her in one arm. And guess what? Not only did Mom use the name I suggested, but The Peanut . . . er, Halli . . . has my hair!

Although I think it's more of a curse than a blessing.

I can't wait for Nona to see her! I already called her and told her all the awesome details. And Nona told me her own good news too. She said that Andrew talked to her (so lucky!) and that "Barney" is actually having puppies soon. So Barney was a horrible name for that dog, just like I said from the very beginning. But get this—the dog's real name is . . .

AMIE!

I could so almost die! I was jealous that whole time of a dog! And I wasn't even really jealous, just . . . curious.

So Andrew is giving one of the pups to Nona—her mom actually said yes to that! Totally unbelievable! I guess Nona's mom isn't as terrified of dogs as we thought. Or maybe she's not afraid of the tiny ones. Who knows.

I asked Nona what she would name her pup. She said, "Lukas." I told her she can't name her dog after her boyfriend and she said, "Watch me."

I guess with Lukas leaving and Andrew not having a crush on other girls (and those boys getting detention for fake-fighting), the boys' room will be a little quieter than normal. Especially since that Bloghead posted a warning about the Blogtastic Blogger possibly having stakeouts near the boys' room.

He obviously reads my blog too much.

Whatever. I have better things to do than stake out out the boys' room (not that I was doing that). For example, the other day when I was leaving school, I heard something. I really wasn't trying to listen or anything, I swear! But any time there's a whisper, my ears perk up. The whispers seemed to be coming from a group of girls huddled together. And it was at the exact moment I was sloooowly walking by! Like it was meant for me to hear.

So my ears just happened to detect part of their conversation as they excitedly chatted about sleepaway camps and summer vacation. Something about burnt-marshmallow wars, water fights, ghost stories around campfires, and total boy drama. Sounds like perfect blogging material.

Hmmm, maybe a summer of sleepaway camp is just what I need. . . .

Secrets from the Sleeping Bag
Another BLOGTASTIC! novel by Rose Cooper, available next summer!
SECRET SUMMER SURVIVAL CASE
CAMP

ROSE COOPER is a children's book writer and illustrator and a self-taught artist. Her artwork can be seen in galleries and at art fairs and festivals. Writing for children gives her the perfect excuse to keep in touch with her inner child and never grow up. She lives in Sacramento, California, with her husband, Carl, and their three boys. You can visit Rose's website at rose-cooper.com.

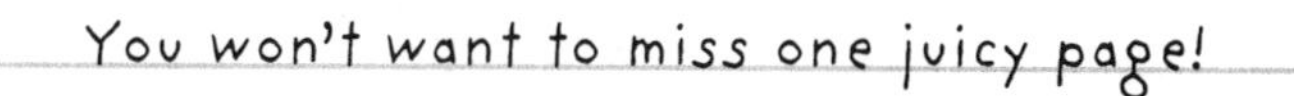